"It's a bomb. Under the driver's seat."

The floor rushed up to meet her ass as her knees gave way again. "Are you sure?" Of course he was sure. He was a whiz of a wizard.

"Of course I am sure." He looked indignant and delectable at the same time. "Would you like me to remove it?" He crossed his legs at the ankle as he leaned against her ready-to-explode station wagon.

"Yes, please." It never hurt to be polite. She made the most of her manners. "That would be most kind of you. Thank you."

All of her blood was pounding through her head as she watched him gesture and mutter. With her eyes open, she triggered her second sight and watched his magic ebb and flow. The colors were wild, blue, brown and a shimmering black. A lovely display of phantom colors as the explosive device was levitated out from under her car to hover in front of it. The instant that it hit the daylight, it began to explode. Xander couldn't contain it.

The bomb was small but deadly as a dome of power encapsulated it. The only problem for her was that it wasn't Xander's power that had wrapped around it. It was hers. A bright sphere of blue, purple and gold. Iridescent and beautiful, they swirled around the explosion and held it in physical and temporal stasis.

Her day was looking up.

This book is a work of fiction. Names, characters, places, and incidents either are products of the author's imagination or are used fictitiously. Any resemblance to actual events or locales or persons, living or dead, is entirely coincidental.

Nexus Chronicles: Gnomes of Suburbia
Copyright © 2009 Viola Grace
ISBN: 978-1-55487-268-8
Cover art and design by Martine Jardin

All rights reserved. Except for use in any review, the reproduction or utilization of this work in whole or in part in any form by any electronic, mechanical or other means, now known or hereafter invented, is forbidden without the written permission of the publisher.

Published by Devine Destinies
Look for us online at:
www.devinedestinies.com

Library and Archives Canada Cataloguing in Publication

Grace, Viola, 1971-
    The gnomes of suburbia / Viola Grace.

(The Nexus chronicles ; book 1)
ISBN 978-1-55487-268-8

I. Title. II. Series: Grace, Viola, 1971- . Nexus chronicles ; book 1.

PS8613.R333G58 2009   C813'.6   C2009-902222-2

Nexus Chronicles

Gnomes of Suburbia

By

Viola Grace

Kristy,
Keycon was the
mini launch. :)
Viola Grace

Dedication

To Mortimer who watches my back yard and to Splitz, who guards my sleep. I love my gnomes. Silent guardians of our begonias.

Chapter One

HER HANDS SHOOK AS SHE PRIED OPEN THE LETTER, AND WITH A squeal of delight, ripped the documents from their enclosure. She flipped through the pages, detailing her sales and gaped at the final figure on the cheque.

It was everything that she had ever wanted. Annabeth Hanover clutched at the precious document that would lead her to the next step in her life and let out another squeal that had the neighbours pounding the walls in irritation.

"I have it! I actually have enough to buy my house." Her giggles and happy dance took her through her tiny apartment and onto the balcony-fire escape. Who could have imagined that selling a book with photos of her own sculptures would be the means by which she got her freedom? *Gnomes of Suburbia* was that very book. A pictorial record based on the rather modern take of garden gnomes in an urban setting.

It was not a best seller, but this third royalty cheque was now enough for her to put a down payment on the house that had haunted her dreams since she first set eyes on it.

Number Thirteen Oak Point Way would be hers, provided that no one had purchased it in the three months since she first turned down the street and laid eyes upon it.

The instant that she had stepped out of her clapped out station wagon and walked up the overgrown drive to meet the realtor, she had known a feeling like none before.

She was finally home.

ANNABETH HANOVER HUNG UP and then stared at the phone in her hands. Her super had just told her that if she could leave her apartment by the fifteenth that he would refund her complete deposit and an additional month's rent. The money would pay for three months of her mortgage at her new home. She would be a fool to miss out on it, wouldn't she?

With a deeply felt sigh, she called her real estate agent and asked her about the possibility of her getting in earlier. "Miranda! Hi. How are you today?"

"Fine, and how are you Annabeth? Getting ready for the big move?"

"Yeah, about that. Is there anyway I can get into the house before the fifteenth? I mean when you showed it to me, it was ready for me to move in. So would it be possible?"

Silence reigned on the other end of the line. "I had a call from the water department, they need to come in to change out the meters and investigate a leak so I am afraid that it won't be habitable for another few weeks. I am very sorry."

"No, no problem. I will let my super know that I am staying until the thirty-first. Thanks for considering it."

"No problem, this is why you should always call your real estate agent before doing anything rash." Miranda's warm tone relaxed Abby as it always did. "No surprises this way."

"Exactly. Well, have a great day and see you on the thirty-first. I can hardly wait. Bye." Her mind was already whirling with possibilities. One kept floating to the surface and she repeatedly shoved it down. Finally, she was alone in the coffee shop with one other patron and still staring at her phone and running the options. When a latte arrived in front of her and Tina nodded to the guy in the back of the shop reading the paper, she sighed, then smiled. "Tell him thank you, he may have just saved my life."

"Yeah you had that look about you. He's a nice guy. No strings attached." Tina shifted off and she was left with a steaming cup of coffee and the same problem that she had had since speaking to Miranda. Abby needed to get out of her apartment early, and God help her, there was only one way. With a shaking hand, she punched in the number and took a long draught of her latte. She winced as the end of the line was picked up. "Hi, Mom? Do you still have an empty garage?"

While she listened to her mother agree to the use of her property, Abby's gaze wandered over to the man who had sent her the latte. When he dropped the paper enough for her to meet his eyes, she sighed in disappointment. Sure he was gorgeous, but he was brunette and brunettes creeped her out, that dark hair and those dark eyes hiding something. The instant that she thought it, he looked up at her, startled. In a flash that left her rubbing her eyes, he vanished.

Seriously, he just disappeared. His paper was crumpled and his coffee still steaming, but he was gone. Just like magic.

Chapter Two

IT HAD BEEN TWO WEEKS AT HER MOTHER'S BEFORE THE WOMAN finally snapped. "How did you manage to fit all of this stuff in your tiny apartment?" Betsy Hanover had as much contempt for her daughter's collection as she did for bits of foil trash on the street. They were pretty and shiny, but she wanted them away from her pristine home. Abby just sighed.

"It's a talent for collection, Mom. I came by it honestly." She simply shrugged and went back inside the house, leaving her mother to take a mental inventory of her pile of stuff. Abby was going to get some breakfast.

Her mother's house was pristine and clean, and cluttered with about five thousand pieces of china from a variety of eye bleeding patterns. Despite the clutter, there was not a speck of dust to be seen, Elizabeth Hanover pursued it as her arch enemy.

This was the main reason that she disdained her daughter's *dirty* hobbies. The fact that sculpting often used real dirt distressed her to no end. Abby simply shrugged it off and kept up her hobbies.

She fixed herself some eggs and toast, settling to read the daily paper. She skimmed over the movie releases, the book releases, got a chuckle out of the personal ads and then moved on to serious stuff. Local crime caught her eye when she saw an eerily familiar room photographed on the page in front of her.

Her old apartment had been ransacked.

The picture showed the new couple's boxes slashed in what the paper was calling one of the worst acts of vandalism they had ever seen.

The new couple was quoted as being shocked beyond belief that their property had been destroyed within weeks of their moving in.

Especially brutal was the destruction of the new bride's collection of dolls and stuffed animals. Not one had been left intact. Abby winced as she imagined the amount of stuffing strewn about the apartment. Her heart went out to the new occupants.

"Hey, Mom! Did you see this?"

Betsy bustled into the kitchen, sweeping away the minute crumbs of Abby's breakfast with a frightening attention to detail. "What, a new toy?"

"No. My old apartment was broken into. They trashed everything that the new couple had. Even the stuffed animals." She shivered as she spoke. Someone was walking over her grave. If she had moved out even two weeks later, those would have been her belongings being trashed. Her precious gnomes would have been at the mercy of the vandal and she wouldn't even have had a chance to show them their new home.

"Too bad it wasn't your stuff. You could have claimed on your insurance and replaced everything." She gave the paper a cursory glance. "It would have been like a home makeover show."

"Are you saying that having a violent stranger trash all of my critters would have been a good thing?" Outrage filled her voice, she could hear it.

"Don't raise your voice to me while you are in my home." Her mother played the victim well. "After I opened my home to you in your hour of need."

"For a tidy profit, Mom. You are charging me to be here, remember?"

Her mother looked shocked. "Only in some of your crafts for Christmas presents."

"My time and effort aren't valuable? The list of stuff you gave me could earn me close to three thousand, Mom. They aren't just *crafts* to collectors."

Betsy sniffed in disdain. "Whatever. You still owe me." She cruised from the room under full sail, as regal in her demands as any queen.

Alone again, Abby muttered to herself, "Fine. But I am leaving my fingerprints on everything." That tiny bit of rebellion would make her feel smug.

Ah well, she only had one more night in this place and then she was off to her new adventure. And she could leave her crumbs wherever she wanted.

It was a damned shame about the new tenants of her apartment though. They had seemed like a nice couple. She hoped they had insurance.

HER ROOM HADN'T REALLY changed much. It was still far too neat, all blue chintz and white oak. Betsy hadn't wanted to encourage her creative daughter any more than necessary. Her room had been kept sparse and utilitarian at all times. The only decorative thing that she had owned was her big book. Abby had found it in the woods and had kept it close to her ever since. It soothed her like nothing else and here it was waiting for her on the desk. Her one steady friend. She surveyed her room and came to the inescapable conclusion that nothing had changed. The window overlooked a spacious backyard and it was sparse but well kept, only one garden shed at the back of the property.

Abby had taken over one of the backyard sheds that used to be there and made it her own. She could see the spot where it had squatted when she looked through the window. Her mother had wasted no time in removing it from the premises the instant that her daughter had moved out. That was sixteen years ago.

Abby had learned a few things since then. Her crafting wasn't a nasty habit, it was a compulsion. She had to make the things that she did, in the manner that she did, or go slowly nuts. It wasn't a hard choice.

Chapter Three

In times of stress, it is completely natural for someone to think of quotes of nostalgic wisdom. This was just such a time.

"A TRUE FRIEND WILL HELP YOU MOVE." ABBY MUTTERED UNDER her breath as she took a load from the moving van to the porch. The movers were doing their part with the larger items, but to empty the truck in under an hour would save her a hundred bucks. So she moved her own limbs as rapidly as possible with every cardboard burden she took up. The pickup from her mother's home had gone smoothly, if under nagging that was still ringing in her ears. Still, she had moved her stuff out in two weeks and kept up her end of the bargain. No boys, no drinking and no crafting in the pristine showplace that was her mother's home.

When she stumbled and almost dropped her box of moulds and casting materials, her breath caught in her chest as the box righted itself and proceeded into the pile under its own steam. "What the hell?" She blinked furiously, but the levitation continued until the box was safely settled.

Abby looked around for some explanation, but her movers were still on their lackadaisical route to and from their truck. They hadn't seen anything.

She checked her watch and swore under her breath. She had five minutes to finish getting the boxes out of the van or she would have to give up her hard-earned cash.

A strange energy filled her arms and legs, she ran back to the truck and began to hoist and drop the boxes into a pile next to the loading ramp.

The cargo area had been half-full, but as her body made the shuttle too and from the edge, she had it cleared in no time. If some boxes seemed to shift themselves, she was sure that it was just a trick of the light, and her hard work. Gasping and glowing ever so femininely in the bright light of the afternoon, she greeted her slack-jawed movers with a tired smile. "It's done boys. You can go now."

"But half the truck..." Bill trailed off as he saw the echoingly empty interior. His voice reverberated in the hollow space. Nothing was left except the moving blankets off her dining room table and a few straps that had secured everything while in motion.

She took a limp and sad looking wad of money out of her pocket, sweat ran through denim so easily. "So that was one hundred for the first hour and fifty for the delivery."

They looked like they wanted to scratch their heads and their butts at the same time, just to cover both points of thought. "Uh, yeah. But did some of your friends come to help?"

"Nope. I am just a motivated mover." She smiled and waggled the folded bills at him. "Here you go."

"Thanks, ma'am. It was a pleasure, and any time you need movers don't hesitate to call us." Bill and Randal tucked in the ramp and closed up the back of the cargo area. With a grunting roar and the belch of diesel, they took their shuddering conveyance and disappeared into the green-canopied pathway that was Oak Point Way.

With the movers gone there was just one thing to do, meet the grass, up close and personal. She collapsed onto her front yard. The grass prickled at her skin and she idly watched a ladybug make its rounds on her thigh as she fought for breath. What the hell had just happened? There was no way that she had shifted all those boxes by herself, and yet, she had. There was no other explanation. At least none that her over heated mind would consider.

As she lay on her back and contemplated the lovely pattern of the leaves occasionally flirting with the sun on the massive oaks in her yard, a shadow crossed her line of site. Huh, the shadow had hands. They gripped her own firmly.

"Hello. You must be Annabeth. Up you go." She was lifted to her feet with a sharp tug and found herself facing the most extraordinary creature she had ever seen. Her head spun and she grasped the woman firmly to keep her balance as the blood rushed back to its proper disposition.

If she wasn't a sceptical person, she would swear that the woman was green. Just a light hint of aqua in her features and a pine tint to her chestnut hair. "Uh, hello. Who are you?" She was quite striking, but she had a stillness to her that Abby found slightly unnerving.

"I am your next door neighbour, Laura. Laura Exner. Feel free to come by and use the pool anytime. Or the hot tub for that matter." Her bright smile invited Abby to smile back and she did so out of reflex, only then realizing that the thought of a hot tub was causing the facial response. She was a little sore from the move. In fact, living in her front yard until her muscles healed was a fantastic idea. Mmm. No more lifting.

"That's very generous offer for a woman you don't even know." She was a little dizzy from being pulled to her feet and she squinted up at her new neighbour with suspicion. Her own five foot six came up rather short with Laura.

"Well, you are single, like arts and crafts and have few friends nearby. Not to mention family."

"How did you know all that? Are you a private detective or something?" It was creepy. She was right on the money. Well, not about the family. Her family had washed their hands of her move the instant that they saw all of her crafting stuff.

"Me? No I own a pet store in town." Laura presented a card that stated *Exner's Exotics—Saltwater fish for your aquarium*. "I just noted your lack of assistance for your move, the single name on all the boxes and the little show of you unloading a moving truck by yourself." She crossed her arms, drummed her immaculate nails and smiled. "You are either the most stubborn individual that I have ever seen or you had no one to help you."

Abby raised a brow, "What about the arts and crafts?"

Laura tapped one of the boxes of marked plaster with her stiletto. "I assume that this is actual plaster and that you don't enjoy hauling twenty kilo boxes for entertainment."

Laughter seemed the only option, "Entertainment it isn't. It's my livelihood."

"Oh? What do you do for a living?" Bending gracefully Laura picked up two of the plaster boxes and nodded toward Abby's new home. "You coming?" The heft of the burden was not noticeable in her stride, Laura must workout.

"Uh, sure." She picked up a box of her own and almost staggered under the weight. "I sculpt creatures and then take photos of them in costume. My first book just came out." She took point and slithered past her deceptively strong new acquaintance. "In here."

Her workshop was one of the larger rooms in the house. She supposed it was originally a formal dining space, but she couldn't resist using the light streaming in through the sliding glass doors.

"Wow. It seems like almost all your boxes are supplies." Laura gave the boxes a longing look. "I don't suppose you would have any finished sculptures handy, would you? I would love to see your work."

Abby sighed and looked toward the front of the house. "Could it wait for another time? It is going to take me a while to finish moving all these boxes."

"Hmm. Would you like some help? One of the other ladies on the street is off today and I think Verne is home."

"Uh, that would be great. Is Verne your boyfriend?"

Laura snorted daintily. "Well, we go out occasionally, but nothing serious. He lives in number twenty one." She flipped out a cell phone and began to dial and walk as she headed back to the curb. It was impressive. Abby couldn't dial and talk at the same time.

Bemused, Abby followed and began a stately shuttle of boxes into her home. In minutes, they were joined by two more inhabitants of Oak Point Way.

This sure was a friendly neighbourhood.

VERNE FISHER WAS CHARMING. A shade under six feet tall, a neatly trimmed beard and moustache in a dark brown hue and his ice blue eyes calmly focussed on Laura the entire time that he was helping with the move. It was the gaze of a patient hunter, the knowledge of the outcome clearly stamped in his eyes.

Seesee Montrose was much more animated and a far better conversationalist. Her hair was a thick mass of braids that framed her delicate and exotic mocha features. Her eyes were a startling contrast, a brilliant violet that met her own with a direct gaze. It was from Seesee that she learned that Verne was a Customs officer who had been sniffing after Laura for eighteen months. What a surprise.

Laura's shop specialized in saltwater fish and tanks, and all the accoutrements for maintaining the exotic creatures. Her face lit up as she described the importance of meeting clients and matching the fish and the tanks with the maintenance level they were willing to give.

Seesee's shop was far more mundane, and to Abby, far more fascinating. She owned a bakery. One of the best in town.

Montrose's Munchies sold cakes, cookies and treats of the high calorie variety. She promised to deliver some of the treats the next time that she visited. Today was for celebrating a new addition to their neighbourhood.

When all the boxes had been shifted into her home and some were being unpacked by the strangers, Abby asked the question that she had been dying to since Laura picked up that first box. "It's very nice and all, but why did you all come to help me move in?"

"I think that that answer needs some tea." Laura was already in the kitchen and unpacking boxes. She had obviously found the kettle as the whistle had sounded earlier. A tray rattled as she led the way into the living room, Seesee grabbed Abby's arm and dragged her along.

"Uh, can I wash my hands first?" Abby was almost digging her heels in as they passed the bathroom.

Seesee had the grace to blush, "Oh, certainly." Her hair shifted almost restlessly but Abby was certain that it was a trick of the light. It almost looked alive.

Verne was something of an interior decorator. As soon as he finished moving the furniture, he had turned to her bathrooms and sorted her toiletries. He was so metro it was scary, and yet he had this weird lumberjack vibe that emanated from him almost constantly. He was an urban warrior with a great sense of style.

She used the pump soap that she used for her hands when they were covered with plaster and scrubbed a lot of the dirt and grime out from under her nails. She would never be able to compete with Laura's immaculate manicure so she was giving up and settling for tidy.

Entering her new living room filled with people who didn't even know her and yet who had helped her move in, she was almost in tears. It was too much. Her day had been more stressful than she could have ever predicted. She was overwhelmed by every emotion she had ever experienced.

"I just wanted to thank you all so much. I am lucky to have new neighbours like you. If there is anything I can ever do for you, just let me know." A tear did manage to struggle from her eye. As it tracked down her cheek, her audience watched with rapt attention. The instant that it hit the floor there was a thunderclap, the walls of the house shook.

"What the heck was that?" Abby was on her feet in an instant. The last thing she wanted was one of the enormous oaks in her roof. The sky was blue and clear. No sign of the ominous noise.

"I am sure it was just a car backfiring." Seesee's voice was reassuring and satisfied at the same time. "Come back and sit down so we can all get to know you."

"That was one big effing car." That made her pause for a second before she sat down. "Uh, if this is about some kind of kinky stuff, I am not interested. I currently don't swing in any direction."

She calmly sipped her tea as she waited for the laughter to die down. Okay, so maybe they were just friendly.

"Sorry to laugh at you, Abby, but that is not the reason that we wanted to talk to you. It has been so long since a new nex...ooof!" The elbow that Verne drove into Laura's side had a bit of force behind it. She glared at him as she continued. "A new next door neighbour moved in. We have a tight little community here and actually enjoy talking to our neighbours. Number Thirteen has been empty for quite a while. If I may ask, didn't you have any second thoughts about purchasing an unlucky number?"

Abby had been preparing for this question since she signed the contract. "I like the number thirteen. It's a prime number. It contains a one and a three. I like those numbers as well. Plus the house just feels right." She looked around at the oak floors and cream walls. "It feels perfect. The second that I saw it, it was mine."

"Excellent. This neighbourhood has needed someone like you. Oh, I am your next door neighbour on your left, in number Nine." Laura nodded to her and smiled while getting her second cup of tea. "I have the only pool on the block so feel free to pop by anytime to use it. Really. Anytime."

"Thanks. That is very generous and kind of creepy, but I don't know how to swim." The shock on Laura's face was almost comical. "I never had the opportunity to learn. Do you know somewhere I could take classes?"

"Yup. My backyard pool. Six o'clock tomorrow night. I am fully certified as a swimming instructor." Her face still showed her shock that an adult could not swim. She was recovering slowly.

"And when you get tired of swimming, I'll pop by and you can get your just desserts." Seesee piped in. "Oh, if you need me for anything I am Number One. On the street, that is, Number One Oak Point Way."

"To get it over with, I am in number Twenty One. Directly across the circle from Laura." Verne didn't sound too happy about that. His grimace indicated that he wanted to be considerably closer, at all times.

The conversation turned to her selection of DVDs and then trailed off as they began to get ready to leave. Their impromptu party unravelled quickly and soon they were out the door, with Abby promising to take swimming lessons. They walked slowly down her sidewalk, murmuring to themselves, and she could only sigh with relief that she had landed in a welcoming neighbourhood.

"YOU IDIOT! SHE DOESN'T know she's a Nexus. She hasn't even begun more than the basic manifestations." Verne hissed it in Laura's ear on their way down to the street. He loved her, but tact was not one of her strong points.

"Well, her vow was more than basic. Did you feel that shockwave?" Seesee was amazed, the power of that tiny gesture had almost caused an animation. But she had to keep her eye on Abby. After all, it was up to Abby to control the expansion of the magic that would be produced. Her hair hissed in annoyance at the restraint it had been asked to engage in and she shook it out to let it free. The braids unravelled in seconds. Tiny snake-like tendrils moved softly in the afternoon breeze.

She didn't worry about being seen. There was only one minimally magical person on the street and she wasn't at home today. Randy was goodhearted, friendly and completely harmless for someone without an ounce of talent, she simply had been born into a magical family. A rare find and a welcome member of their close little community.

Her hair danced and caught the breezes, revelling in the new magic that had been spilled in the neighbourhood. She liked Abby. The new Nexus was a genuinely nice person. Now, if she could get control over her growing talents quickly, it would be much easier for her to join the magical community at large. For her sake, Seesee hoped that she was a quick study. Wild magic would not be tolerated indefinitely. The council would only leave her alone as long as she was under control. If she lost her control, she would lose her liberty.

Chapter Four

Dreams were Abby's weakness and the reason that she loved to get her eight hours of sleep. She loved the experiences in dreaming, even if she couldn't remember them. She only wished that the people she met in her dreams were as real as they seemed.

Tonight's dream was no different.

Everything was pastel. A huge crescent moon hung over a scene that reminded her of her new backyard. The huge oak was moving on its own, creatures that were surprisingly human jumped out of the river to wave at her and she wandered around this magical place touching and sniffing everything. It all seemed so bright and attractive.

Awash in her magical world, she held in a giggle as her gnomes strutted themselves across the green. Harby was exceptionally cute as she pranced in his leather and vinyl finery. Bitsy was controlling the others by herding them into formations that had endless sighs and laughter coming from their creator.

The gnomes were joined by the memory of creatures that she had made to sell to supplement her income. Dolls, unicorns, dragons and beasts that had no name populated the yard.

Their amusing capering held her attention for what seemed like hours until she felt a strange presence enter her little Eden.

It was a man, or at least the shadow of a man. Power seemed to come off him in waves as he approached her. He had no features, but was simply an outline of a masculine nature.

"So how are you liking your new home, Abby?" His voice was deep, rich, and she wanted to listen to him read the phonebook.

"I like it just fine."

"And your new neighbours?"

"They seem friendly. I think I could like it here." She looked around and noted that her gnomes had gotten into a keg of beer. Two of the buggers had crawled onto her moon and were singing songs while dangling from the crescent.

A drumbeat started in the background. "That's weird. My mind usually doesn't have a soundtrack." The beat shifted into an upbeat tango. A band kicked in and soon her mind was alive with her creatures dancing and the gnomes singing off key.

"I brought it along. Shall we dance?"

She looked up at Mr. Shadowface, "I don't know how to tango."

"Just trust me."

"Dude, you don't even have a face."

He held out his arms. "Does it really matter? This is your dream after all."

He had a point. Abby took a deep breath and stepped into his arms.

The first steps were awkward, but after he caught her a few times, she realized that he was a lot more substantial than he looked. They started to move faster and her head was whirling, it was only during the final dip that she had a chance to catch her breath.

It finally hit her and she had to ask, "What are you doing in my dream?"

He bowed formally from the waist after setting her on her feet, "Just welcoming you to the neighbourhood, Abby. Care for a waltz?"

She shrugged and embraced him again. A dance partner was a dance partner. Who cared how he got into her mind?

Chapter Five

WHEN ABBY WOKE THE NEXT MORNING, EVERYTHING WAS QUIET. She felt calm, serene, but still, it was too quiet. The sounds of the city were gone. Winnipeg wasn't huge, but it was still larger than the tiny town of Sargent. She immediately got up and started to make some noise, anything to break the silence. When she had a cup of coffee in front of her and was seated at the counter of her kitchen drinking it with a CD playing in the background, she could finally relax. And think.

Ah, nothing like moving into one's own home. At long last she had a place to call her own. No upstairs neighbour stomping like an elephant and no one behind a wall who liked to have domestic arguments at the top of their lungs. She had never felt right with the noise and clatter of the city, but here, she could breathe.

The peace and quiet might take some getting used to, but she loved it as much as it disturbed her. Taking her coffee with her, she went into her workroom and started to unpack. First her big book and then her gnomes.

Having their little cheerful faces around her would make her feel more at home. She took them out of their crates one by one and smiled as she lined them all up. Harbinger was her bondage gnome, kitted out in black leather, zippers and studs. She had even put a zipper running up his pointed gnome hat. His name had been a play on words. A sex related gnome meaning *things to come*. She hadn't been able to pass it up. His creation had spurred on the wave of creativity that had spawned the others. Even Bitsy.

She checked to make sure that the tutu of the ballerina gnome was intact. It had come loose in transit so she brought her over to the worktable that Verne had set up for her and got to work on repairs.

Hours passed before she looked up and it was something making noise outside that had distracted her. Specifically something knocking on her door.

Wiping her hands on her jeans, she blinked and stumbled to the front door. Holy crud. If this is what the church canvassers looked like in this neighbourhood, she was going to convert. She didn't even care if squirrel shaving was one of the requirements. Sign her up.

She finally remembered to open the door and smiled at her visitor. "Uh, hello?"

"Hiya. I just wanted to introduce myself. My name is Alexander Desmith and I live next door in Number Seventeen." He held out his hand for her to shake. His palm was warm, firm and he held her hand carefully. He almost seemed afraid to touch her or harm her by the contact. That was a little weird.

"Hi. I am Abby. Uh, Annabeth Hanover. I just moved in." She was babbling. She couldn't help it. Blonde wavy hair, baby blue eyes and a body that had to work out at least four times a week. He was amazing to look at.

When he smiled, he was even prettier. "I know. Laura told me to present myself or face her wrath." No fair. He had dimples and a strangely familiar silhouette. Ah well.

She smiled back, her heart racing and blood pounding through her veins. "Laura is rather intimidating, isn't she? She has demanded that I learn to swim." Something occurred to her, "I'm being terribly rude, would you like to come in for coffee?" She remembered that hers was a few hours old. "I was just about to put on a new pot anyway."

"That would be great. Having Laura pounding on my door the instant that I got back from a business trip was a little intimidating." That mind-smacking grin was back and she could almost feel the air around her trembling with energy.

She found herself backing away from him, down the hall and all the way to the kitchen. She was so going to slap herself once he had gone.

She went about the mechanics of making coffee. "What do you do for a living if you don't mind my asking?"

"I am a consultant. I sweep in when things are going wrong and try and sort them out." He perched his chin in his hands as he leaned on the counter. "I know it's vague, but each situation is different."

"Sounds reasonable to me."

"Turnabout is fair play, what do you do?"

She couldn't help it, her lips twisted in a smirk that she tried to hide. "I have recently discovered a small but interesting market for books featuring gnomes in urban settings."

"Gnomes? Like that one in the corner there?" He gestured over to Harbinger who was occupying a corner of the kitchen.

"Huh, I thought that he was in the workshop. I must have moved him while working on Ruffles."

"Ruffles?"

"The ballerina gnome." She stood. "The coffee will take a moment, Alexander. Do you want to see them?"

"Xander, please. And I would love to." He scooted past Harbinger and looked a little abashed. "Are they all dressed like...uhh."

"No, he is my only BDSM gnome. The rest are all based on other costumes and themes." She smiled at the small marching row of gnomes on the floor.

"Introduce me, please." He bowed formally to the gnomes and Abby wasn't sure, but she would almost swear that they acknowledged it somehow.

"All right. This is Mitsy, the female boxer gnome. Notice the small boxing gloves?"

"Yep."

"Next to her is Splint. He has those crutches because he was trying to look under Ruffles's tutu. Ruffles is the ballerina gnome on the table over there. She was damaged in shipping so I have been repairing her this morning. Now she is good as new."

"Is that one..."

"Naked? Yeah, his name is Skint. But I did put a lettuce leaf on him. And last, but definitely not least is Bitsy, my dwarf gnome. Don't even ask me how that one worked out. I think I was short on clay or inspiration that day."

"They are all fantastic. Where did you get these ideas?"

His genuine appreciation warmed her. It was so rare to be able to show her creatures to an appreciative audience. Let alone one that made her heart pound in her chest.

She was so screwed.

"WHERE DID THAT LITTLE bondage gnome go? Did you move him?" Alexander looked around at the corner that the little beast had previously occupied and blinked. He was definitely gone.

"No, why?" Abby came around her worktable and she bent low to look for her model. Her butt was definitely nice. Her hair was a little shorter than what he normally preferred, but she was a bundle of goodwill and energy. Definitely his type.

When she had greeted him at the door, he had been surprised to see her face, it was so open and girl-next-door. There was even a sprinkle of freckles across her nose. Her hair was a golden brown that shifted from dark to light as she tilted her head and it framed the soft green of her eyes perfectly.

It was her mouth that made him pause. It shifted and twisted with every mood. One moment sensual, the next pursed, then pensive as she began to work on her gnomes. It was her mouth that was the insight to her moods. He could watch it forever.

He had been expecting someone much older, or at least someone more serious. Abby may have a good soul, but it was steel in her heart that would let her survive as the newest Nexus. She was just too soft. Bringing new magic into the world was the task for a strong soul.

She was still only beginning to create the magic that was spilling into the world, but it had begun to manifest. Training her was going to take a lot of courage and self-control on his part. Her ass was fantastic.

"HARBINGER, WHERE THE HELL did you go?" Abby called out and looked around. She felt silly, but she always talked to the gnomes once they had faces. She felt that the moment they had eyes, they had a soul. It was that moment when they came to life, in her opinion. It was also the reason that she made the faces last.

There was nowhere for Alexander to have moved him and he couldn't get around on his own so when she felt a tug on her jeans and looked down into the eyes of the thigh high bondage gnome, she screamed and jumped back. Right into Alexander.

"Do you see what I am seeing?"

She found it ironic that he was asking her. Her own mouth was opening and closing without any sound making its way out.

"Harby? Is that you?" A frantic nod from the gnome and she felt her butt hit the floor hard as her knees buckled. Abby simply stared at her creation come to life.

Harbinger took a few steps closer and then stuck his hand out to her. She looked at him for quite a while, then took his diminutive appendage in her hand. She shook it and a bright smile crossed his face under his beard.

He jumped up and threw his tiny arms around her neck. She hugged him back, absorbing the warmth that was emanating from his small body.

The hug lasted just long enough to start making her uncomfortable. "Okay, Harby. That's enough." He smiled and nodded as he stepped back. She moved to push herself back to her feet and stopped. She stared at the little bugger that she had just released and he grinned back, unrepentant.

The damned gnome had unhooked her bra.

"Xander, did you just see Harbinger come to life?" She felt she had to ask the only other human in the room if she was hallucinating.

"Yes, I did indeed. In fact, he is currently trying to strip your ballerina, Ruffles, was it?" He gestured toward her workroom and she darted forward to stop Harby from tinkering with the delicate composition of the repaired tutu.

"Harby. Knock it off. Go comb your beard or something." She picked him up and moved him out of the workroom, this time she closed the room behind her to protect the other inhabitants from his busy fingers. Hopefully he couldn't reach the doorknob to get back in. She really needed a moment to sit.

Shaking as the enormity of what had just happened hit her, she moved to have a seat on the couch. Her head hung down between her knees as she tried to absorb the fact that one of her sculptures was trying to climb into her cupboard.

"How could that happen? How is that even possible?" She shook her head and kept it down.

"Well, he absorbed your magic and it animated him. It really is not that complicated."

Horror covered her features, she could feel her skin pale. "What do you mean *absorbed my magic*? I don't have any magic."

"I beg to differ. You are a Nexus and by your very existence magic will enter the world." He seemed formal, as if his declaration was some kind of judgement, handing down a sentence that she wasn't going to be able to dodge.

"What the hell is a Nexus? And why are you talking like you know what's going on? I don't even know what's going on." The high-toned shriek that she heard could not possibly have come out of her mouth, but the sore bits of her throat let her know that she owned the scream.

"I would tell you to calm down, but this is exactly what I am referring to." He gestured to the workroom door that now had light knocking on the other side. She heard more than one little arm hammering at it and closed her eyes.

"This can't be happening. Magic doesn't exist and gnomes don't come to life." She repeated it both out loud and in her head, but it didn't stop Xander from opening the door and letting out her gnome companions.

She was immediately swarmed by the crowd of tiny creatures who all wanted to give her a hug. Her heart was pounding, but the calm hugs of the gnomes stilled her frantic mind. A cuddle with Ruffles, a snuggle and a mussing of her hair from Mitsy, who also helped Bitsy up onto the couch so he could wrap his little arms around as far as he could. Skint was the only hug she had to debate returning. What had possessed her to make a nude gnome? Everything she touched was naked flesh.

"How are they doing this?" She turned her head to ask Xander and her gaze ran smack into his smiling eyes.

"They aren't. You are. Your fear or excitement or adrenaline is causing you to release magic. I can feel it spilling out every time you move." He took one of her kitchen chairs and put it in front of her so that they would have direct eye contact. "I am here to help you get control of your triggers. So that you can summon extra magic at will and not leak it everywhere."

"Leak it?"

"When you don't control the dispersal, the effect will be to animate objects, cars, houses, anything that you are near when your power runs amok."

"Then why didn't my coffeemaker come to life?" Now she was just being picky.

"Your gnomes were more personal to you. You had a connection to them and the power flowed through that connection."

That made a horrible kind of sense. She did think of the gnomes as her children. Sort of. They were certainly her own creation, no wonder she would be tied to them.

In the mean time, what was she supposed to do with them? Hmm. Her backyard was fenced, would they go out? "Come on guys, you can get some fresh air and enjoy yourselves. Knock if you want to come in, okay?" She moved slowly through the small bodies and opened the sliding door onto the deck. With tiny squeals of joy, there was a gnome stampede and she and Xander were alone once again.

She turned to him with a welcoming smile. "Get out of my house."

"What?"

Silently she walked calmly to the front door and opened it. "Get out."

Chapter Six

"ALL RIGHTY, LAURA, I AM HERE FOR MY FIRST SWIMMING LESSON. Please don't drown me." Digging out a swimsuit had not been easy, but her stepsister's insistence on beaching herself with Abby as an audience had finally come in handy. She had a suit that she hadn't worn in three years. Luckily, it still fit.

"Oh, I have no intention to drown you, in fact, it is why I asked you here. I want you to be able to swim. Especially with that wide river in your back yard." Laura looked fantastic, as always. Not a hair out of place. "Now, shall we begin your instruction?"

Laura turned out to be quite an excellent instructor. She went over the basics at poolside and then took her slowly to the shallow end. "It's a saltwater pool, so don't worry about chlorine, and I will jump in if you need me."

"Uh, okay. Let me know how I am doing." Slowly, and with a sense of dread, she took a firm grip on the ladder and lowered herself one step at a time. Every one of her nooks and crannies was now water cooled. The salt water had more buoyancy than she had anticipated, it was easy to stay afloat. With only a few corrections to her technique, she was soon making her way slowly but surely from one end of the kidney shaped pool to the other. "Can I stop now?" Her limbs were exhausted.

"Sure, I have some drinks and snacks ready." Laura waved her over. "Come on out."

Shaking with fatigue, she clumsily moved up the ladder and onto the concrete tiles that rimmed it. She flopped down like a beached dolphin. Swimming was exhausting.

"Come on, Abby, you did great. Here's a nicely warmed towel."

Laura was being very kind, but as Abby lunged up to grab the fabric, it snagged on Laura's leg and when she stepped forward, she fell headlong into the pool.

The shock of the splash of the water was second only to the shock of seeing the blue shimmering tail breach the deep end and propel her host to the shallows.

Smiling apologetically, Laura slid out of the pool effortlessly and immediately resumed her legs. She had been wearing a sarong, so Abby was spared the full mermaid on land experience.

"Uh, you weren't supposed to see that yet." Laura retrieved another towel and began to dry her hair.

Slightly numb, Abby mimicked her movements. "Yet? There was some kind of schedule?" She finished fooling with her hair and wrapped the towel around her.

"Uh, well. There are a few things that you need to be informed of, but we aren't sure how far along you are." She looked frustrated at having to keep to such a vague description.

"Well, if I didn't hit my head, I brought six statues to life this afternoon. How is that?" She felt a little bit smug as Laura's eyes went wide, but then she realized that it was because Seesee had come into the yard.

"So, Abby. How are you enjoying the neighbourhood?" Seesee was chipper and carrying a box of something that smelled amazing.

"Well, apparently I exude magic, animated my garden gnomes and my next door neighbour is a mermaid." Abby was still not on her feet and she blinked rapidly. "Anything that you would care to add?"

Seesee looked her over carefully. "You need to get some sugar and some food into you before you get any more news bulletins from Oak Point Way."

Mute, Abby went to the table that was set with snacks and tucked in. There was a sampling of fruits, crackers and cheeses. When Seesee unloaded her box of goodies, there were also miniature cheesecakes and tiny strawberry shortcakes.

The only sound was a steady munching, occasionally broken by *oohs* and *ahhs*. When her belly was full and her hand no longer shook when she picked up the teacup, Abby decided that it was time for a few pointed questions.

"So how many magical creatures live on Oak Point Way? Are there any others like me?" Abby's question broke the quite camaraderie of hungry women.

"Like you? No, there are no others like you. In the magical community, you belong to the most rare of all the talents. The rarest creatures. I suppose that Xander has told you that you are a Nexus?" Seesee's direct stare held Abby hypnotized. Her hair was moving gently in the wind, except there was no breeze. The air was silent.

"Yeah, but I still don't know what it means. I can bring my sculptures to life, but can I do anything else?" Since she was trapped through the looking glass, she may as well enjoy the experience.

"You brought your gnomes to life? Cool!" Seesee's enthusiasm was contagious. The ends of her hair lifted and began to writhe in the air. She wasn't wearing braids today and her wavy tresses still hung in locks. Moving locks.

"I am not imagining that. Your hair is actually moving, right?" Abby blinked slowly, not sure if her eyes were playing more tricks. She almost hoped that when she woke up, this wouldn't be a dream. At the same time she was terrified that it wasn't and she would wake up tomorrow with her gnomes in her room looking at her.

"You are going to need an ophthalmologist appointment every week if you blink that much every time you see something new. You are in a whole new world now, Abby. And there is no way out." Laura's pronouncement sounded sinister and light hearted all at the same time.

"You mean, I just can't stop doing this? It won't just go away?" Her frustration was evident. "It isn't just a phase?"

Seesee and Laura shared a long look. Seesee finally spoke. "I know that it's hard, but once the magic starts to flow, there is no stopping it. I am a gorgon by birth. When my hair came alive, I freaked. I did everything I could to keep it under control, even a buzz cut. Finally, I accepted that it was part of me and that it was my own magic that animated it. So what I feel, it feels. It can also pick up lightweight objects and occasionally a large one. So it's really handy when I go shopping and bring in the groceries." As she spoke, her hair unfolded from behind her head and reached a length that covered her to her rib cage. Her hair was swirling happily around her and Seesee's smile was brilliant.

"There is only one moderately talented person on the street and you have already met her. Randy is an unpowered woman raised in a higher level magical family. She is also a kickass Real Estate agent."

A strange new feminine voice rang out, "And she is standing right behind you."

"Hiya, Miranda! It's nice to see you again!" Abby's greeting was genuine, Miranda had been a calm and knowledgeable source for the steps that Abby had to go through to get her house. She had helped her navigate the endless documents and insurance forms that had led to her ensconcing herself here on Oak Point Way.

"Nice to see how well you are fitting in to our little gathering, Annabeth. How have the ladies been treating you?" Miranda moved smoothly into a chair and poured herself a glass of wine. It was turning into quite a ladies night.

"Everyone here has been most hospitable. It is the friendliest neighbourhood I have ever been in. I just wish that the circumstances were different." She shuddered lightly and felt a small tingle. Abby flexed her fingers and then wove them together in her lap. "This is too much weirdness for me."

Laura gave her a straight stare that had her squirming in front of the other magical women. "You will have to adapt to it. It isn't going to go away."

"But why me?"

Seesee looked calmly at her. "Why not you? Let me guess, you were creative early in life, always making things with your hands or writing?"

"How did you know?" She didn't think she had shared any of her childhood memories with them, but maybe they could read her mind? Yet another chilling thought for her to cling to.

"It is the hallmark of a Nexus. You create magic and life even before you are able to share your magic with others." The snake-like locks on her head hissed in agreement. They flared out and formed patterns around her that had them in hissing giggles.

"If it wasn't for Nexus' being born every few generations, wild magic would cease to exist. It's wild magic that enables the fairies, pixies, gnomes and sprites to exist. They generally congregate around an area where a Nexus once resided." Laura and Miranda were letting Seesee do all the talking, and no wonder, her hair was hypnotizing.

"Does your hair always move like that?" Abby gestured to the rhythmic sway that the impudent strands had taken up. She was pretty sure that it was responsible for Laura's sudden silence.

"Knock it off!"

Abby blinked, but then realized that Seesee was talking to her hair.

"Sorry about that. It is one of the problems with being a gorgon. The hypnosis is what happens when I am not paying attention. I have lost more boyfriends that way." She shrugged. "And when they realize what has happened I have to deliberately enthral them to make them forget."

"So that is an example of magic being out of control?" That weird tingling feeling was growing within her again. Her skin felt electrified, like a static charge before the big zap.

Laura shook her head and laughed lightly, apparently this had happened to her before. "A minor one, yeah. But I suppose that it is a good way for you to start out. Anything larger might spook you more than you already are." A light hand on Abby's shoulder was meant for comfort, but the shock of power that leapt from Abby to Laura was enough to slam her backward.

Laura's tail was really very pretty and very full, however Laura looked very disconcerted at the change that had come over her without her will.

"Oh my god! I am so sorry Laura! I don't know what happened." Abby was on her feet and humming with the surge of adrenaline that the transfer had caused. Ironically, she now felt more charged than she had before Laura touched her.

"Seesee? Can you roll me into the pool? I seem to be stuck in this form." Laura was very calm. And rather iridescent. There was a shine to her that hadn't been there the first time she changed. "Oh, and throw that fish mobile from next to my backdoor into the pool. I don't think that they want to be out of water for a while."

As one, the dry ladies turned to see the swimming fish on the wind chime actually swimming. Abby backed away from the activity. It was too much.

The fish were trying to swim while still on strings, Laura was stuck in her mermaid shape, Seesee's hair was going wild and Miranda was looking at her like she was a freak.

What else could she do? She ran home and hid under the covers.

Chapter Seven

THE GNOMES TROOPED GLEEFULLY INTO THE BACKYARD, CHORTLING amongst themselves as they enjoyed their first moments of life. They chuckled and hugged as they gathered in their yard, rejoicing in their sentience and mobility.

As the eldest, Harbinger took it upon himself to begin organizing their community. Names were on the agenda as he thought the names of some of his brothers and sisters slightly silly. "Ladies and gentle gnomes. I know that our mistress has named us according to her whim, but would any of you care to be known amongst your brothers and sisters by another name?"

Bitsy stepped forward. "I am Bitsy. Our mistress named me and it is the name that I will answer to when a human calls. I will be proud to carry the name I was given until the day that my life drains from me, if it ever does. My true name is still within me and that is enough." Bitsy stood proud. The others slowly nodded. Their names had been chosen by the one who brought them life. It would be a dishonour to reject them.

"Now. Do we stay and serve the Nexus or go into the world and make our way?"

"What would we do?" Ruffles asked.

"Where would we go?" Skint chipped in his own query.

"How would we get there?"

"What do we know about this place or the physical world really?"

The debate raged all day. Bitsy wished to stay with the mistress, but Splint argued that their lives were theirs to live. They need not wait on her to earn their keep. She had created them intelligent and able-bodied. They could fend for themselves.

"Enough!" When they fell quiet again, Harby continued. "It is obvious that we need to become familiar with this world, and at the same time, the Nexus is coming into her power. She needs us here. We do not wish her to run afoul of anyone before she has grasped her control."

Bitsy nodded. "I will not leave her, but what do you propose, Harbinger?"

"That we use this opportunity to both protect the Nexus and to learn about her world. We will use her yard as a base of operations and expand our knowledge of the world from here. After we know more of this place, we can discuss it again."

His brothers and sisters nodded. "What do we do first?"

"Well, the sky is darkening. I was thinking of following the road and seeing where it leads." With giggles of agreement and enthusiastic grins, Harby and the gnomes took to the open road.

Their feet pattered quietly on the pavement and, each time a car passed, they ran for the shrubs. They may have just stood still and pretended to be statuary, but it was a hard thing to do when their instincts screamed at them to run.

The town was huge to their eyes. Mind you, to them all human creations were enormous. They took in the town square, the grocery, the home and garden center and the tiny computer repair shop.

Mitsy peeled off from their group and began to examine the door to the grocery store. Her brow furrowed as she eyed the locks. "The Nexus needs breakfast tomorrow. She has not had time to shop. How do we get inside?" Mitsy was being practical. It was a good thing that she was, none of the others had even considered the physical upkeep of the Nexus herself. If she lost physical power, their lives might be endangered as her power sought to return to her body.

Harby was a little embarrassed, but he tackled the task with all the enthusiasm of a career felon. After a few minutes of searching around, he found an entrance to it. The round holes in the ground with the metal cover led to drains that were smelly, but they connected to every building in town. The gnomes were just the right height and width to make their way through their dark expanses. They had the key to every business in town, it led through the sewer.

It had to be magic because after they finished their crawl through the tunnels, they didn't keep the stench on them. Nor the filth. They were as clean as the day they had been made, but they were not going to bring any items out through the depths.

Shopping was managed when they actually figured out what the Nexus would want in the morning. It was called a cookbook. Bitsy memorized three while Splint and Mitsy went with Skint to the home and garden center to find some nice plants and tools for them to begin sprucing up their home base. The Nexus's home was serviceable, but it lacked a certain style. She needed a little help in that department and they were just the gnomes to help her.

Harby and Ruffles did the *shopping* with deliberate attention, following Bitsy's instructions to the letter, a modest but thorough compilation of groceries that would satisfy the nutritional needs of their mistress. Her health was important. Without it, they may cease to exist at any time.

With their items carefully stored in the recycled bags that were offered, they trundled to the door and with a sharp flip from Bitsy on the lock, left the grocery store. Moving through the doors took Harby and Ruffles a lot of effort, but they managed. With the bags in front of them, they headed to the edge of the common green.

"SO WHAT DO YOU think, green around the edges and pink in the center?" Mitsy was diligently selecting appropriate pots and setting them aside. Creating a color scheme in the yard may help the Nexus gain control and keep her calm. With all the power that was going to be flying around when she grasped her talent, she definitely needed a place for meditation.

"I think some blue and purple would also be a good mix. The Nexus does not seem to like yellow so we may want to leave that one out."

Splint offered that opinion with a slight sniff. He was being incredibly prissy for a garden gnome, especially one on crutches. "Where did Skint go?"

Mitsy sighed and kept selecting soothing choices for the garden. "He is trying to arrange transport for the garden materials."

"What kind?"

"I have no idea. He is looking for something in the *kids cars* section. I don't know what exactly that is, but he seems to." She shrugged and selected a few more bedding plants. Each was chosen with deliberate care, nothing was too good for the Nexus. It was quite a few minutes until she heard a high-pitched whine that preceded Skint by ten seconds. When he rounded the corner, Mitsy yelped in shock. It was a small vehicle with enormous tires, just their size, and it was bright pink.

"Isn't this fantastic? It's called a *Barbie Car*, and there are three more like it in the kids section." His pride in his discovery was obvious as he tooled around the concrete, making lazy figure eights in his new vehicle.

Mitsy edged around it daintily. "How does it work?"

"It runs on batteries that we can recharge at the Nexus's home."

"How do you know all this?"

Skint puffed up with importance and crossed his arms over his chest. "I am a boy."

She opened and closed her mouth repeatedly. Nothing that she could come up with could challenge that statement. "Fine. Where do I get one?"

Skint cackled evilly. "Hop on."

She delicately took the seat beside him and kept her gloves up in case he tried anything. His naked thigh touched hers twice, but that was as far as she let him get. A light tap on his arm with her glove had them swinging toward some shelving so she refrained from punching him hard until they reached their destination. She made a mental note, *don't hit the driver.*

"Wow. You were right. There are more of them." She perused the selection and smirked with glee. "I want that one."

"Hey! I didn't see that one. I want it."

"Tough. Stick with pink. It looks good on you." She strode definitively to the vehicle that announced itself as a *Batmobile* and tried it out. It took a bit of trial and error, but she worked it out. "Go get Splint so that he can drive another car and meet me back at the plants. I am going to get familiar with this vehicle."

Mitsy tooled the car around the home and garden center. She determined the cornering radius, the top speed, and with a bit of chain, some bolts and an under car creeper, she determined load capacity. They had enough power to start transporting things home.

It was time to roll.

It took some managing, but Mitsy got their small caravan arranged with four vehicles, each couple towing a line of creepers and wagons to bring their supplies home. The groceries had been collected and added to the Batmobile and Jeep combination with the Barbie car and another Jeep bringing up the rear. High-powered flashlights were mounted on the front of each vehicle and made the perilous journey down the side of the road a little bit lighter.

They kept their conversations to a minimum. The new skill of driving required concentration and the thought of being seen was in all of their minds as they made their way home. The small vehicles were not built for off-roading, but they did a respectable job.

They were almost to the turn of Oak Point Way when an oncoming car caught them in its headlights. The car slowed to a crawl, its occupant staring at the little parade that they had formed. When the driver accidentally steered into the brush, they made their move. Hitting the accelerator and swearing, the gnomes directed their conveyances into the safety of the shield around the street to the cul-de-sac.

The driver of the car, a woman who was looking rather perturbed at her loss of vehicular control, was left looking at the three potting plants that were left behind in the sudden swerve. From behind the bubble, Mitsy looked back and sighed. She loved those plants. Perhaps they could get some more the next day.

Chapter Eight

Something was different. This morning when Abby woke up, the house was not silent. There was clattering and clanging going on and she bolted out of bed and into the kitchen. And almost fainted. It was real, it was all real, or her mind had snapped big time.

Stationed at the coffeemaker, the skillet and the toaster were gnomes. The little beasties were making her breakfast. After the shock of seeing every chair she owned made into an access walkway for them, she had to admit that they were neat cooks.

As she sat at the counter on one of the stools that her brood had not pressed into service, she felt the first stirrings of embarrassment run through her. She was mortified that she had run from the gathering, but she hadn't known what the hell had been going on and was just tired enough to go into full panic mode. Bitsy patted her hand in commiseration as her walked by, setting the table. It almost made her smile.

"So fellas? Did anything else come to life last night?"

He had to have been waiting in her living room because Xander's voice made her jump three inches to fall heavily back onto the stool. "There were reported incidents of missing lawn ornaments and footprints in the dirt for a three mile circumference around Laura's place." He crossed his arms and scowled at her. "What the hell did you do last night? You generated enough power to set ceramics marching all over town."

"I don't know what I did. I wish I did know. Is Laura still stuck with her tail?"

"Yes. And we are going over there after breakfast so that you can try and reverse the power shock that you gave her." Xander moved to sit next her and she scooted over a bit.

Oddly enough, in his role as her teacher, she didn't find him sexy at all. His chastising tone had her sulking and feeling like a dog that peed on the carpet. "Okay. I know that I did something last night to build up the charge, mind you, I don't know what it is. How do I bleed off the magic without contact?"

"You don't. But you find an item to discharge the power into. In the past, Nexus's have used rocks, knives, gems, belts, armour, small items that can be worn on the person. This lets you bleed it off as it generates, instead of reaching critical and popping."

She mulled it over as a cup of coffee was delivered to her the way she liked it. "But what would I do with all the bits and bobs that I charge up?"

Xander rubbed the back of his neck and pondered his next statement. "In the past, the Nexus has been taken into custody by the leading council of the time. Whether it was dragons, witches or warlocks heading the council."

"Taken into custody?" Scrambled eggs and toast with three strips of crispy bacon and strawberry jam were now in front of her. Bitsy was the final position of the assembly line and he just walked it over to her. She knew where Xander's discussion was going.

"A polite term for kidnapping, but it did generate a lot of new magic, wild magic, for the world."

"And that is the main concern, isn't it? That I will produce the magic that everyone is so desperate for." She dug into her food out of reflex, but stopped halfway to thank her gnomes. "Hi guys! Thanks for all your hard work this morning. But I only have one question...where did the jam come from?"

Harby walked to stand next to her and looked at her seriously, it took three tries, but eventually his mouth opened enough to say, "We found it for you. We will find anything for you."

"Thank you." She smiled and went back to her plate through the tears in her eyes. Her creations could speak now and she felt like a proud parent. A second plate of food was dropped in front of Xander and he looked at it in surprise. "Eat it. You don't want to insult them. No telling what they will do."

"No kidding. They love to be busy. Have you seen your backyard yet?" The amusement in his tone set her nerves on full alert.

She took a deep and shaky breath. "Can I finish my breakfast before I have anymore shocks?"

"Of course." He tucked into his own food, heavy on the pancakes and bacon. Apparently the gnomes paid attention to preferences. A lot of attention.

The instant that they finished, the plates were whisked away and conveyed to Skint who had stayed away from the frying, but had no problem cleaning up.

She sighed with satisfaction, she could deal with anything on an full stomach. "Okay, let's try and freak me out in the backyard, shall we?"

Xander grinned at her and her earlier disinterest went right out the window. God, he was handsome. And he probably saw her as no more attractive than a battery. How depressing.

Together they moved through the halls that had been buffed to a high shine, and when she stepped out onto the deck through the sliding door, she gasped and it was long moments before she remembered to breathe.

Her original yard of two days earlier had been fenced in on two sides with the back of the yard open to the river. Her only large item in the yard was the mighty oak that had lived there for a few hundred years at least. She wasn't going to mess with that.

Now, there were tiny gardens in all kinds of shapes and sizes running through her yard. The odd part was that flowers were implanted in the ground and seemed to be enjoying their new home. A tidy stack of green potting cases gave her the final clue to her new beautiful yard. "They have been raiding home and garden centers, haven't they?" She covered her eyes with her hand and tried to think of all the ramifications.

"I don't know, but they have been busy. You may want to keep an eye on local news." He wandered into the floral expanse and asked her, "So what else would you want?"

"I think I would need a meditation space and organize the colors into soothing pallets. And some decorative stones to charge up and use for balance." She walked around the tiny paths that left just enough room for her feet. "The plants got blasted last night as well. They are humming with energy already and I haven't even touched them."

"You have now created a yard full of magical flowers. You should be proud. I have never even heard of such a thing." His hand moved to take hers and she shied away. She backed up until she was touching the oak and, with a relaxed sigh, emptied her charge into the tree. It could take it.

"There. I no longer have a charge. Let's go visit Laura." The leaves rustled as she turned to take Xander's arm and she deliberately did not look back at the tree that now had a full burst of magic. Part of Abby was still trying to pretend it wasn't happening.

The other part was enjoying the feel of Xander's arm under her hand. The warmth of the muscle under her fingers sent a tingle of recognition through her. If her hunch was correct, she had just found one of her triggers because she had started to power up once again and his muscles were responsible.

"I'm back here!" Laura's voice called out through the fence and they headed for it. A wave of Xander's hand and a tingle of magic later and a door appeared in the forty foot fence where none had existed before.

Abby was in a hurry to apologize. She stumbled up the steps leading to the pool and knelt at poolside. Laura's skin was practically pearlescent. She looked lovely, but also unhappy.

"Look out!"

Her warning came a second too late as a snarling wolf tackled Abby and rolled her onto the grass. He pinned her down with his jaws at her throat and growled.

With a choked voice, she tried to calm him. "Hi, Verne. I know that it looks bad, but Xander is going to help me undo what I did to Laura."

A blue nimbus surrounded the wolf as the Warlock levitated the werewolf off her and into the hot tub.

"Aw man, it is going to take me forever to get all that fur out of the tub." Laura flicked the water with her tail and leaned back to relax against the edge of the pool.

"You could have called to warn me." Xander was irate now. He helped Abby to her feet and dusted her off.

"Is Verne stuck, too?" Oddly enough, being attacked by a werewolf was not as shocking as it would have been three days earlier. Perhaps she was going crazy.

"Well, he hasn't shifted back since he kissed me last night after you left." She looked a little abashed. "He must have absorbed some of the magic."

"With all that wild magic flying around, it's likely that that is what happened. But he may want to keep in mind that no creature here wants to kill our new Nexus. She is providing us with the first large magical boost in almost seventy-five years." Xander hunkered down next to Laura and met her gemlike gaze. "We need to keep her alive and well to keep the magic coming."

"I'll remind him. Now, give Abby the instruction she needs." Another impatient swish.

It was now her turn to be the center of Xander's attention. "All right, Abby. Since we don't know what your trigger is, I want you to concentrate on the feel of your own magic. Just keep quiet and recognize the taste and rhythm of your power."

She felt a little silly, but she knelt on the other side of Laura and closed her eyes. She breathed deeply and tried to recapture that tingle that spurred her magic to life. She thought of things that made her happy, then things that made her sad, and when she finally got around to things that scared her, she had her answer. It was adrenaline that made her magic live. She examined the properties of the energy that her body was releasing. It was green, purple and silver. A fantastic swirl of color. "I've got it."

His voice came from far away, "Good, girl. Now look at Laura with your eyes still closed. Do you see your energy?"

She looked over the mermaid from head to toe and saw a layer of her fabulous colors over the greens and blues of Laura's own magic. "Yup."

"Good. Call it back to you, slowly."

She tried several methods to recall it, but finally, it was pulling her own power into a large ball and hovering it over Laura that did the trick. Her magic was narcissistic. It wanted to be with itself. When Laura was clean, she *looked* over at Verne and saw a light trace of her magic on him. She floated the ball over and her power leapt home.

"There. I have it all. They are clean." She opened her eyes and looked hesitantly at the werewolf first. He was back in human form and reaching for a towel. Then it was time for Laura.

"Thank you, Abby. I know that you didn't mean anything by it. But the power that you have isn't compatible with existing races. It can create a boost, but it isn't designed to be permanent." Laura was climbing out of the water and Verne shoved Xander aside as he covered her with another towel.

"I didn't even know what I did. Only that it zapped you and brought those fish to life. How are they enjoying your pool?"

"Eh, they are pretty good company for stuff that was handcrafted in Bali. But they are rather cliquish." She winked at Abby.

"I am so sorry. I didn't mean to." Abby was hanging her head when Laura padded up to her on wet feet.

"Sweetie, I am positive that you didn't mean to. You will learn control with time. But I hope for my sake that it is soon, 'cause I really want to give you a big hug. You could use it."

"You can't, I am holding a charge." Her arms had wrapped themselves around her torso without her volition and she looked up sorrowfully into those wonderful blue green mermaid orbs.

"I know. Now, I believe the next lesson that Alexander has for you is to harmlessly discharge your magic into something else. Something not moving." An encouraging smile lit the mermaid's face.

A wan, hopeful smile crossed Abby's features. It was that or bawl like an infant. An inanimate object it must be.

Chapter Nine

Harbinger was pleased, breakfast had been a fantastic hit. "Good idea, Mitsy. The Nexus was very happy with the breakfast and the yard. Can everyone feel it?"

When his siblings nodded their assent, he was pleased. The Nexus was sharing her energy with them passively and they were all benefiting by a form of passive transfer, and being her creatures, the benefits were making them smarter, faster and sneakier.

Their speed was increased as was evident when they managed to set the kitchen to rights in a matter of minutes. Juice was prepared for lunch or whenever the Nexus was thirsty and they scampered outside to work on the yard.

It needed a lot of work. The previous owner must have neglected the balance in the soil shamefully, creating that balance was first on their list for the evening's activities. The refurbished laptop was useful as the mermaid had an unprotected network at her house and they simply hacked her signal. Details of the world around them flowed in a matter of seconds. They had a question, it was answered as soon as they had the right way to phrase it.

"I love this *Google* thing. It's amazing." Bitsy was in charge of their Internet access because he seemed to know what to look for. He was pretty good at it, too. They had taken paper from the Nexus's house and made lists of items that they specifically needed for the house and garden to be at their best, all compiled from the information that they had gathered.

It was a really long list.

The yard really needed some work.

When Bitsy came to him and stated that they needed some additional assistance for the Nexus in case the magical inhabitants of the neighbourhood got out of hand, he thought it was a splendid idea. The smallest gnome immediately went to a pharmaceutical website and started to shop.

The others were starting the tunnels that would carry them into the heart of Sargent and throughout their neighbourhood. The ultimate in discrete transportation. No one would see them on their little shopping trips again, as soon as the conduit was complete. This life thing was going to be fun.

Chapter Ten

"ABBY, WOULD YOU COME WITH ME PLEASE?" XANDER GESTURED for her to precede him as he moved toward the gate between the properties. He kept a careful distance between them, but stayed close enough to let her know she was not alone. It was cold comfort, but she would take it.

Her own energy was a steady push against her. With no outlet, it wrapped around her like a smothering blanket. An itchy, suffocating blanket.

She stumbled once or twice and whimpered as no one came to her aid. Xander merely waited until she righted herself, then continued to shepherd her into her own backyard. Obviously, touching her was out of the question. That dampened her enthusiasm for his body slightly. Only slightly.

"The rock at the far end of your yard should be a safe target." He kept his arms at his sides as he followed her to the back of the property and waited for her to discharge her magic.

Suddenly she felt slightly exposed, "Could you turn around?" It was as if he had asked her to disrobe.

"What?"

"Could you turn around? I haven't done this before and don't want anyone to watch. Passing along energy seems...personal." Her blush could have sparked a fire.

He gave her an astonished look, but turned his back to her anyway.

The tree in her yard looked oddly patient as if it had been waiting for something for a long time. "Am I supposed to use the oak?"

"No, the stone. Oaks are alive. Who knows what would happen?"

Oops. Talk about belated information. She needed a Nexus manual. *How to not be a power flinging idiot in 10 days.*

The oak was calling her, pleading with her to share her magic. She altered her path slightly and then was within reaching distance of the rock and the oak. One needed her, the other didn't. She chose.

"It isn't working. Why isn't it working?" She winced a bit at her own tone, the bark under her hands merely waited.

"You need to relax into it, let the power flow away from you and into the rock. May I show you?"

The faintness of his tone left no doubt that he was still facing away. What an honourable guy. Sucker. "No. I need to work through this. No peeking." Relax and let the power flow. Deep breathing aided her relaxation and with her mind's eye watching her power, she let a trickle of power into the tree and in seconds, she felt it drawing the magic from her with a raw hunger that she was unprepared for. Her hands could not leave the rough bark, but her mouth was free. "Xander, I have screwed up here!"

His voice mercifully grew closer, "You know, I had a feeling that you would do something like this." He still didn't touch her, but was sitting next to her, shaking his head. "Relax and let it take the surplus. It will take a few minutes, but it will stop when it senses your regular life force."

With the closeness of his body, her magic flared into a second dose for the tree. This was going to take a while if he didn't get his hotness out of her field of vision. She could just about imagine how much harder it would be if he wasn't wearing a shirt. Oh lord, there was another wave.

It was unending, and when Xander finally clued into the little fact that the tree was not letting her go, he made the mistake of trying to pry her away from her wooden companion. The pressure of his body behind her as he pulled at her arms to facilitate the releas caused a pulse in her body that gave the tree enough energy to stroke her hair gently with a low hanging branch. That just wasn't right.

"Okay, that is really creeping me out. Xander, can you back up a bit?" Abby hastily added, "Not all the way, just let me get my left leg out."

He seemed to understand what she wanted and moved aside with one arm around her waist, keeping them in contact. Carefully, she extended her leg and reached out with her sandaled foot. As her toe connected with the rock, a massive discharge of magic pulsed through her and into the stone. She also reached out to draw her own energy from the tree and that is when it let her go. The instant that it freed her, Xander pulled her back and they tumbled to the ground with him on top. Oh, this was so going to mean another trip to that rock.

"Hah. I knew that there was a way to do it." She was smug and more than a little impressed. He felt as hard as he looked.

He cocked an eyebrow at her. "What, precisely did you do?"

"What, weren't you watching?" Hmmm. Was that a wand in his pocket or was he happy to see her?

"Yes, I was, but I still don't know what you did." He was propped up on his elbows.

The fantasies that romped through her head were now guaranteeing another trip to the rock. "Uh, I improvised?" A bright and cheery smile that felt more like a grimace. She almost sighed in disappointment as he moved off her and sat next to her on the grass.

"Seriously."

"Seriously, I drained my magic through the rock. Then started to siphon my own power back from the tree. The tree let go, then you jerked me through the air and here we are." She gave a small shrug.

"You learn quickly."

"I do try. Whatever this is, I want to get a handle on it quickly. The sooner I control it, the better." Her own words rang in the air between them and she shook at the truth of it. She really did want to control this thing that was running through her, it surprised her. She didn't even know that magic was real until yesterday and now she was a living fountain of the stuff.

"Don't worry." With a caring move, he reached out to take her hand. The shock of energy that rushed to him with the skin-to-skin contact made his eyes flare electric blue and seconds later, he leaned forward to take her mouth with his. For a slow kiss, there was a ton of energy between their bodies, lips and tongues in action, but the more power she generated, the more rushed through the circuit until Xander broke from her in a daze. "Abby, I thought you discharged your power." His tone was not accusing, but his eyes were still glowing.

"I did. It came back." She was practically flying apart at the seams. Xander had not taken enough energy to drain her and she really needed a stiff one. A rock, that is, not anything else. She rose to her knees and stumbled over to the rock, this time staying clear of the oak as she dumped the power into the rock.

"Xander, I am just going to sit here until you go home. I am a little out of control tonight and want to sit here and meditate for a while." And to not think about how you felt against me. Definitely not that. She sent another wave of power through the stone. She watched him go and part of her was jumping up and down in frustration. She was pretty sure that if she could get her hands on him, they would end up between the sheets.

Apparently, power was an aphrodisiac. Now if only she could bottle it, she could make a fortune.

Chapter Eleven

HARBINGER SKIPPED THE ONLINE SHOPPING IN FAVOUR OF KEEPING AN eye on the Nexus. Not once did he feel a tug on the energy that bound him and his brethren to her.

She was gaining control at an amazing pace.

He was interrupted in his musings by her return to her property. Quickly he called out, "She's coming back. Hide!" Harbinger himself tucked a shrub around his body to conceal the paler expanse of his face and hands.

He heard scrambling in the yard and the slide of the back door so he knew that they had made it to safety. Or to a less obvious watching position.

The Nexus certainly did not need to see them with the *borrowed* laptop. She had enough on her mind.

Chapter Twelve

Locking the world out used to be a simple matter of not answering the phone. But now, with a gaggle of gnomes alive and in her house, Abby was having a few difficulties ignoring the last few days.

While dawn cheerfully tumbled through her window, the gnomes were taking turns knocking on her door. Each knock was as individual as the gnomes themselves. Three hours passed with their tiny fists knocking and she ignored them by dragging a pillow over her head.

Overnight her optimism had morphed into panic. What was she doing? These people were nuts and there was no way that the gnomes she had carefully assembled were alive in the world and doing her housework. If she stayed in bed long enough, it just might be true. It was only when a human knock and voice came through the door that she moved the pillow.

"Abby, are you okay in there? We need to talk."

Grimacing, she sat up and ran her hands through the mess that used to be her hair. "I'm up."

Seesee continued as if she hadn't heard anything, "All right, I know that yesterday was rough on you. We had hoped that you would be able to ease into the whole Nexus thing, but you weren't and here we are. We know that you didn't mean to supercharge Laura, but that is why Xander offered his services. As an actual magic user, he has a far better idea of the control techniques needed than the rest of us do."

Abby calmly listened for a while and then announced, "Give me ten minutes and I will make my appearance."

The shower ensuite to her room had never been so welcome. A tiny bit of privacy in an overrun world. Her body welcomed the water while her mind took an opportunity to leave her alone. No thoughts of magic, mermaids or sex were allowed while she showered, and it was only as she towelled off that she noted that all sounds in the house had ceased.

Bemused, she applied lotion to her skin and took her time selecting her clothing. Today was a day for matching undies. Bright blue and black lace and satin hugged her body snuggly as she worked the bra into place. Ignoring her face and admiring the fit of the clothing in the mirror, her mood lifted.

The jeans and t-shirt were her comfy favourites. The warm and soothing scent of her fabric softener relaxed her another notch and she padded barefoot out of her room and down the hall to the kitchen. She braced herself to confront her madness.

Her madness had brought a friend and chocolate croissants.

"Well you look rested at least." Miranda was helping herself to some coffee and enjoying the pastry.

"I tend to sleep when I am under stress." Her socks made no noise as she joined them.

Randy poured a cup of coffee for Abby as she moved into the open chair across from them. Seesee's hair loaded her coffee with sugar and cream, the tendrils moving gracefully in the morning light. It was creepy to watch a hank of hair stirring a spoon in the bone china cup, but neat all the same.

Randy said, "That's how Xander takes his coffee."

How the hell would she know? The green monster of jealousy was hopping up and down at the thought of Randy pouring coffee for *her* man.

"That's nice. Why are you two here?" She set the cup she was sipping at down with a thud.

Seesee took the lead. "We are here to answer any questions that you may have about the magical community. Well, not all of them, but anything that you can think of and that we can answer."

"Seriously? I can ask you anything?" Abby was almost delighted and Seesee's hair twitched in reaction.

"Anything."

"Okay, I had this crazy dream that I had magical talents, my gnomes had come to life and that my neighbours were magical creatures from myth and legend." She sipped her coffee as the other women giggled.

"Well, Abby, magic is real. Your gnomes are in the backyard, you supercharged Laura and Verne, and my hair is folding your napkins." She crossed her arms and they enjoyed a snicker. "Any other questions? Feel free to ask."

So she did. She quizzed them about unicorns, leprechauns, dragons and gryphons. Three were real, one was fake. The leprechauns had been invented by a Nexus centuries earlier and had died out. He had only made them male. It had been hard for them to mate, but they had really tried. It was a blot on the magical community.

All magical creatures with enough power could transform into a human format, even the unicorns. Most magical creatures bred within their own species, strictly to conserve magic. No one wanted to water down the minimal magic that let them engage in their transformations.

"That makes sense. So what do you guys need me for?"

Randy fielded this one, "The magic is running out. Intermarriage is weakening magical bloodlines and fewer and fewer mages and creatures are being born each year." She smiled ruefully. "I am living proof. The only member of my family who can't turn on a light with the flick of a finger from ten feet away."

"Wow. Do you get along with your family?"

"Of course. Now that we are no longer children and they have ceased playing Hansel and Gretel with me."

"I haven't heard of that game, what does it entail?" Seesee was curious now.

Randy took a hefty slug of coffee. "Well, the magical kids take the non-magical ones into the woods, set a disorientation spell and run away giggling while the lost child goes out of its mind with panic."

Abby and Seesee looked at each other, if her face was anything like the gorgon's, the horror that she was feeling was all over it. "Oh god. I am so sorry Randy."

"Hey. I made it to adulthood, didn't I? And all of my cousins have apologized many times over in the last decade." She shrugged and grabbed a cookie. With her experience ringing in the room, the other two were quiet.

Abby's mind was racing. Was magic a good thing if it caused that kind of prejudice? Was there any way to keep people from abusing it?

"Abby. Bad people will always do bad things. Magic doesn't make you evil, but it doesn't make you good either. You will be what you are. No matter what."

The calming voice of the gorgon slowly began to sink into her mind. You will be what you are, no matter what. Words to live by. Abby nodded to herself and reached for another cookie. Munching at the chocolate chip that seemed made by angels, she worked at her next question. "Why did this happen to me? I mean, why didn't a Nexus appear in the magical community at large?"

The two invaders of her home looked at each other as if trying to communicate telepathically. It seems that they came up empty. "I think you will have to ask Xander that one. Nexus's are things of legend, creatures of myth so rare that they appear only once or twice every five hundred years or so. The last one was only seventy five years ago, but he died in the war."

Abby had a giggle at that one, "So I am a creature now. Good to know."

"I didn't mean…" Seesee's hair went wild with confusion. It was picking up cookies and rearranging them on the plate.

"I don't take offence to it, Seesee. I am just not used to being a rare anything." She reached out to touch the gorgon's hand and her hair calmed.

"The fact that you can laugh about this lets us know that you may just adapt to your situation." Randy looked relieved.

"Has that been a problem in the past? A Nexus not adapting, I mean."

"Do you want the honest answer?"

"Yes."

"They tend to go mad. Most had been restrained and confined by various magical factions and the confinement drove them insane."

"Is that what the plan is for me?"

"No! No. I mean, that is why we are all here at Oak Point Way with you. It was a way to have representatives from a variety of magical races here so that no one organization could squirrel you away."

The shock that she felt reverberated through her with a thud. Her coffee mug slipped from her hand as she had been preparing to take a sip and her mind went blank with shock.

"Abby? Abby, are you all right?" She could hear their voices, but it was if they were miles away.

The whole neighbourhood had been seeded with magical creatures, for her benefit. Or for their peace. Whichever one it was, her brain felt like it was going to burst or her stomach was.

She bolted to her feet and out the patio door, only vaguely registering the gnomes doing more gardening. She ran hell bent to the rock and laid her hands on it, dumping the magic that had risen with the adrenaline. As the blessed relief of removing the charge filled her, she looked over at the oak that seemed to be looking at her wistfully. She addressed the tree directly. "Look, I am not going to let you suck me dry again, but if you can shift your roots like you did when you tripped me, you can touch the rock and get the magic. I will feed it and it can feed you. Okay?"

She didn't know if it mattered, but the oak rustled happily at the idea and she left it to work out its method of contact. Relaxed, but still a bit tense, she returned to the ladies who were waiting for her on the tiny deck. "Where were we?"

Chapter Thirteen

THE LITTLE MEETING DETERIORATED AFTER HER EPISODE. SHE REALLY couldn't think of anything else that she needed answered or at least nothing that they would be able or willing to tell her.

The gnomes were nowhere to be seen and she only half-heartedly worried about where they were and what they were up to. This was her perfect moment to go explore her new town and the people within it.

The drive was abominably short, she could probably have walked it in fifteen minutes. It gave her no time to think so she did a few passes of the town square, which actually seemed to be more of an octopus, main streets radiating from the center. The streets between the arms were lined with tiny boutiques and the mother load. A grocery store. She needed toaster waffles in the worst way.

Parking in the small lot in front of the store she exited her beloved station wagon and grabbed one of the well-used carts from the lot to transport her booty in. Her shopping booty that was, her butt hadn't been in a shopping cart in over a decade. She twisted to check it out. Nope, it wasn't going to fit any time soon.

She laughed at herself as she pushed the protesting cart into the store to the interested looks of the other shoppers. She gathered her spoils and headed for the checkout.

The checkout clerk greeted her. "You are new in town, aren't you?"

"I am. I just moved in this week." She gave the middle-aged woman behind the counter a bright smile. "Carla, nice to meet you. My name is Abby." She read the nametag and extended her hand in welcome. The handshake was a welcome contact for Abby, no magic was transferred and it was simply a mark of normalcy.

Carla continued the checkout process and kept chatting, "Where are you living, Abby? Our town has some fantastic views and amazing houses."

She paid for the bill on the electronic display. "I live on Oak Point Way. It's a great street." She kept her smile on her face right up until Carla dropped her toaster waffles.

"Are you insane? Get out of there, weird things happen there. Inexplicable things."

"Um, the house is paid for so I won't be going anywhere. And the neighbours are friendly." She found herself defending the street and its inhabitants and realized that it was how she actually felt. She fit in there. One more freak in the freak show. "What kind of weird things?"

"Dogs howling at the moon, but only at the moon. The fishing there is ample, but there are no fish in that river, except in that one spot."

"That seems normal for dogs, but just good luck for the fishermen." Retrieving her waffles, she loaded them into the cart herself.

Carla seemed nonplussed and rallied with, "Well, I wish you luck and welcome to Sargent."

With a heartfelt, "Thank you," and a smile, Abby moved her cart out the door and took her precious supplies to the car.

Time for her second stop.

Montrose's Munchies was a block away from the Sargent Grocery and the parking area was almost completely full. She squeezed her car into place and then darted into the shop. She thought she would only be a minute, but the line-up in the shop was incredible. The heady scents of yeast, sugar, chocolate, berries and cream filled the air. It was enough to make her an addict.

She was waiting her turn in line when Seesee saw her, her hair bound by a net, and gestured for her to take a seat in the small snacking area that was the right hand side of the shop. As she approached from the front, Seesee approached from the rear and two patrons at a table rose and left as if by magic. "That was cool," escaped her lips as she sat across from the gorgon.

"What was? Oh that. It's a basic spell that lets me clear the place at closing time. After all, I am the owner." It was a sparkling grin that reached over the table and warmed her heart. She was welcome here. There was no doubt.

"All righty, I need some details from you." Without preamble, Abby blurted out the question that had been haunting her for days, "How do you deal with it, the magic I mean?"

"You just do. You need to either reject it completely or embrace it completely. There can be no halfway."

Now she had to ask the question that she hadn't dared to contemplate before, "What would happen to my gnomes if I rejected it?"

"I don't know. They might survive, but the energy that animates them might drain off or be drained by a warlock trying to gain the extra energy." Seesee was giving her a pitying look. "They would not survive long without you, but they would simply revert to the statues you created."

Abby sat in thought for a while, Seesee let her have the silence. It seemed as if all the chatter of the busy bakery was miles away. So she could let her precious little guys and girls be picked off one by one or she could suck it up and embrace the insanity that was rapidly becoming her life. "I have noticed, their energy is slowly changing color." She had been wanting to ask someone about this.

"I don't know enough about the animation, you need to ask Xander that one. As well as the details of the Nexus' of the past."

A slice of cheesecake was placed in front of her. "You truly are a wonderful hostess, Seesee. I have to ask, is there a man in your life?" That question came unbidden.

Seesee blushed to the roots of her considerable hair. "Well, there is someone, but he is hardly ever around."

"Oh, who is it? Dish."

"His name is Miklos, he is one of the guardians of Oak Point Way. No one can pass him during the night and make it to you with hostile intent." Her eyes became dreamy, small tendrils of her hair curling and uncurling.

"I thought that there were more houses than the amount of people I had met."

"There are two guardians at the entrance to the lane. They were installed first to secure the area and the rest of us moved in after that."

"How long ago was that?"

"Five years."

"For five years you have waited for me?"

"Waited for you here. The councils have been debating the method of your introduction for thirty years."

Wow, major stalker time. "They felt when I was born then."

"Yup, and have been keeping an eye on you ever since."

"Fantastic." She smashed the residue of cheesecake crumbs ruthlessly with her fork. "I always wanted to be stalked by magic users. It makes a change from the usual nutcases that engage in that sort of activity."

Seesee sighed and started to tidy up the plates and cups on the table. "They didn't stalk you, they just kept an eye on you until you came into your power."

"Fantastic. They were checking to see if I was ripe yet." All right, she was sulking, it was hard to miss. Her bottom lip came out and she crossed her arms defensively. Yup, she was feeling hard done by, all right. She needed a hug.

"You need to discuss this with Xander. He has far more information of the council's activities regarding you than anyone else." Seesee was now looking distinctly uncomfortable with the questions she was asking.

"Well, thanks for the cheesecake, it was fantastic." Abby rose from the table and impulsively leaned forward to give her a hug. There was only a tiny bit of power transfer and Abby was pleased with herself. Every bit of control she gained was precious.

"You are welcome. Come back anytime. It usually slows down after lunch so I would be glad of a break if you happen to want to chat or just get away from your critters." She was earnest.

With her gaze aimed at the sugar-filled display case, her voice sounded a little petulant, "Can I just come in for cookies?"

Laughter lit Seesee's face and made her look like a cheerleader with amazing hair. "Of course you can. I am working on some new recipes and I think you just might just qualify as a beta tester."

"It's a deal." With her heart a bit lighter than when she walked in, Abby headed back to her car, belatedly remembering that she had frozen waffles in the backseat.

She reached back from the driver's seat and touched her groceries. She blinked in surprise when she found them still cold. A quick check of the clock in her car and she giggled in surprise and a bit of shock. The whole visit with Ms. Montrose had only taken five minutes.

Driving home, she tried to come up with a clever excuse to talk to Xander and came up empty. She pulled up in her drive and immediately the car was swarmed by gnomes. So were her legs. She limped to her front door with Bitsy firmly on her ankle. The gnomes had the door open and were running a mini relay from her car and into her home. Teeny little butlers, they put her shopping away with a maze of upended boxes, stepladders and chairs. She had to watch in amazement. There was a circus act in her kitchen.

Bitsy was slowly crawling his way up her leg and she reached down to scoop him up. They had a nice cuddle as the rest of the troops handled the dispensation of her purchases. She finally turned to the tiny gnome in her arms and asked, "So did you guys have a good day?"

All the small faces turned to look at her and beaming grins broke out around the room. It was at that moment she realized that she had never addressed her creations directly. A part of her heart broke as they gathered around her and she sat on the ground to hug them all. She greeted them all by name. One by one. Even Skint got a full on hug, while Harby got a smack on his leather bottom for unhooking her bra again.

She was a Nexus and these were her creations.

Now she just needed to find out what that meant. Off to Xander's she went.

Chapter Fourteen

SHE STRAIGHTENED HER HAIR BEFORE RINGING HIS DOORBELL and waited. She admired the tidiness of his yard and the panels of stained glass in the door she was facing. Abby was just about to examine her nails for chips when the door swung open to frame Xander. "Hiya. I have a few questions that I need to ask. Is now a good time?"

"That is one question already." He smiled.

Her pulse sped up. Magic began to pound in her veins and she ruthlessly calmed herself.

"Come on in."

"Thank you." She followed his tight ass and meandered through a home that was packed with antiques. "You know, no straight man should have this many antiques." It popped out of her mouth without notice. Her blush could probably have sparked a fire.

"It's my job."

"What?"

"I uncurse family heirlooms and objects that have been deemed dangerous to the public, both magical and non." He escorted her to a living room with walls lined with portraits and tables covered with objects. "Until the council assigned me here, it was how I made my living." Two glasses of lemonade floated through the air at his gesture, one into her hands and one to his.

"Well, you would have been able to make a fortune in the hospitality trade." She sipped at the drink and found it pleasantly sweet. Curiosity dragged her gaze around the room and she burst out laughing as one painting caught her attention. "Why is there a clown painting in here?

How cursed could that be?"

He leaned forward to grip a palm-sized object from the table. "You have enough magic in you to use this. It is a viewer that I use in my work. It will show you the last time that the curse was activated." He rose to put it in her hands.

She studied it for a moment before setting her glass down and moving to the ridiculous portrait on the wall. The clown was the standard pose, his mouth open with laughter, his nose ridiculously large. She fumbled for a moment with the object in her hand and finally managed to open it. It was built like a large pocket watch, but the large case was completely crystal and the face was a mirror. "So I aim it at the object and look into the mirror."

"Exactly. It will show you the details of the curse involved."

"Great." She aligned the reader with the portrait until she could see the image in the mirror and nothing happened. She twisted her lips, focussed and let a tiny bit of her energy leak into the object. The show started.

It was Laura Exner. The clown in the painting had been watching her for some time. It was only after the move to Oak Point Way that it was able to make its move. It was out of the painting and very hungry. Laura smelled so good.

It followed her down the hall and when she wasn't looking, it lapped at the back of her thigh, looking for a taste to match the fabulous smell. She did and a light nip was next. If only she hadn't screamed, smashed it in the head and locked it in a cupboard. It could have had its first good meal in ages.

"*Abby. Abby, close the mirror.*" *The voice seemed so far away and she was trapped in the cupboard.*

A sharp jolt to her hand and the viewer snapped shut. Abby blinked in astonishment at what she had seen, felt and heard. "Holy crap." He leaned over her and took the viewer from her hand. Contact was minimal, but she still managed to keep her power to herself.

"I am surprised that it took you that powerfully."

He still kept his hands free of her as she wobbled to her feet and that act of separation made her grit her teeth. "I had to jump start the mechanism, it may be a little stronger now until you work the charge off it." She settled back in on the sofa and took another slug of the lemonade. "Who knew that a seal could be that angry?"

He was putting the viewer back and turned to her in shock. "A seal?"

"Yeah. It was a seal's soul trapped in that painting. A small magus sealed it in there after he found the seal almost dead on the beach. He then had a clown painted on the treated sealskin. He wanted people to be as scared of clowns as he was." She relaxed back and let the images she had seen wash over her. It was a small child's frustration and humiliation that drove him to create that painting. That he had control of enough magic to do it was just another tool for his plan.

"Seriously? A child did that?"

"Yeah, in the late sixties or so."

"Do you know who it was?"

"No. But with the upped charge, you should be able to investigate. And the reason he attacked Laura was that she smelled a bit like a piece of herring. What seal could resist?" She kept her eyes closed as she heard him pick up the viewer and move to the painting again.

A few short moments later he closed the tool with a snap. "Son-of-a-bitch. It was so simple and yet I couldn't see it."

"I am betting that it happens a lot with older mechanisms that rely on magic. But back to the reason I am on your couch. I need to know about what I am." She didn't have any room to put her feet up on his coffee table so she kicked of her shoes and curled her feet up on the couch.

"You are a Nexus."

"Yeah, but why did the council put all of you here?" This question had been bugging her. "And who the heck is on the council anyway?"

"The council is a group of elected officials from the differing magical races that have survived to modern day." He answered the second question first and crossed his own legs in the lotus position on the other couch.

Oh, he is limber. This has possibilities.

"The last few times a Nexus has been found, it has been drained dry by whoever found it and has died shortly after. We didn't want that to happen to you."

"We? Who is we?"

"Your new neighbours here on Oak Point Way. Each of us volunteered to be here as a type of an honour guard. If you can learn to control your dispensation of magic, you will live a long and healthy life."

"And if I don't?"

"You will sputter and burn out like a candle and there will be nothing we can do to help you. You carry the seeds of your own survival or destruction within you."

Abby took a deep sip of her lemonade. "Wow, that is a heavy conversation killer. Okay. The next question is, why is the energy signature on my gnomes changing color?"

"Really? So quickly?"

"Uh, yeah. So. what is doing it?"

"As living things take on your energy, they convert it for their own use. The more they live, the faster they change. The tree for example will metabolize the energy that you gave it and your magic will be irretrievable from that point on."

"Okay. So as long as it is still my energy, I can pull it back?"

"That is the theory. I don't know of any cases where the Nexus was able to do it extensively though. That is why you need the training that I am offering you."

She sighed heavily. "What exactly would this training entail?"

"Every morning when your energy is at its peak you will come over and I will give you exercises to enhance your control over your energies." Xander rose and moved to a side cabinet, the drawer that he opened yielded a seven-foot strand of pearls. "These pearls are a good outlet for your extra energy. You can fill them up one at a time and use them to relieve the overflow to prevent accidents like the one that struck Laura."

Abby wrapped the pearls around her hand and hefted them. They were not light. "I am supposed to haul these things around with me?"

"Well, they will give you a place to put your extra energy. It's your choice." He crossed his arms and scowled.

How could she not find that sexy? Her power ramped up again and she filled three pearls in a few seconds.

Then three more as he stated, "I want to see you first thing in the morning, every morning until we get this under control."

She would like to see him first thing in the morning, after they had spent the night tangling the sheets. Five more pearls. "Fine. I will be over here first thing in the morning tomorrow."

"Excellent. I look forward to working this out with you. I will be here to help you out as long as it takes." He took her hand in his and looked deeply into her eyes.

Ten more pearls. Oh, to hell with it. She jumped forward and locked her lips with his. It was just as fantastic as the first time, but this time she had him at a disadvantage and he took a moment to react. He reacted with passion and she was halfway through the necklace before she was able to break the contact. "Wow. Okay. We can't do that again. Or we can't do that again today. But I would definitely like to do that again. But not when we are working on extending my expiration date."

His grin was devilish. "Done. The instant that you are firmly in control of the power, we have a date."

She extended her hand and he shook it. "We have a deal. What is your official job title by the way?"

He was escorting her out and he gently pinched her backside as he gave her a light shove out the door. "I am the Safety Warlock. Do you feel safe?"

"Nope, and I can't wait for our date." A wink and a quick peck on the lips and she was skipping back to her house. This place was definitely becoming more and more like home.

Chapter Fifteen

DAY ONE OF HER OFFICIAL NEXUS TRAINING WAS NOT OFF TO A GREAT start for Xander. He really should have asked her how early she liked to wake up before pounding on her door with a cheerful, "Abby, it's time to start your training."

Even her gnomes looked at him with horror as she struggled down the hall and into the bathroom for a shower.

Then he decided to pound on the bathroom door. "We don't have time for you to take a shower. Come on and let's get started."

Bastard. Apparently the thought of her naked under all that hot water, soaping herself slowly was an image that he didn't entertain. Bastard.

Her ablutions took their regular amount of time, but by the scowl on his face, Xander had been waiting two eternities for her. "Abby, I wanted to get started this morning."

She tucked her towel firmly around her and pattered back to her bedroom, "Xander, morning lasts until eleven fifty-nine AM. Chill. And tomorrow, tell me what time you want me there and you won't have to come get me." She turned just as she was entering her room to get dressed. His eyes did not meet hers, they were fixated somewhat lower. Huh, he was an ass man. Handy to know. "Oy. Move the eyeballs higher, Safety Warlock. You might get a crick in your neck if you keep staring at my ass."

His blush was cute but it was paired with a knowledgeable gleam. "You have four minutes to get dressed and then I am coming in after you."

As tempting as that was, she shut the door behind her and slid into the clothes that she had put out the night before. She had a feeling that Xander would be an early riser and she didn't want to be caught unprepared. He still managed to surprise her though.

Her sports bra was yanked unceremoniously over her head and, with a practiced shimmy and a few good adjustments, she was tucked in nice and tight. Just what she wanted if she was working with a hottie. The pressure cut down on the obvious nipplage.

A baggy sweatshirt guaranteed her lack of noticeable arousal and her jeans snapped and zipped with the finality of a chastity belt. No nooky today. She was declaring her body a nooky-free zone. But just today.

At the four-minute mark, Xander opened the door and was treated to the sight of her in the most saggy, shapeless clothing that she owned. Down to the trashy sneakers and slouchy socks.

"Good lord. What happened to you?"

"I got dressed." She fought her smile.

"It looks like your clothing ate you."

"I am just trying to keep my mind on the task at hand." She sashayed out of the room and slapped his tush lightly as she passed. "You may want to try it."

Chapter Sixteen

"I WANT YOU TO CONCENTRATE. FOCUS ON YOUR ENERGY. LOOK WITH your inner eye."

She was currently squinting at him with the one eye she had open. "I can see it. What next, oh Sensei?"

"Do you know how to trigger a burst of magic? How to fill your body with the charge until it is overflowing?"

"That sounds like an orgasm."

"Hush. Be serious."

"Yep. I am at the ninety percent mark now."

"Can you discharge the magic in the air around you?"

"Now you are getting kinky." She was in the lotus position and had a great view of his thighs as he concentrated on watching her magic ebb and flow in the air around her. He was seated on an elevated dais in front of her, which put his crotch right in her line of sight. Wasn't a bad view.

"Do you think you can be serious for just a moment?"

"Okay, but make it fast."

"I want you to release your energy into the room in a violent burst."

She took a deep breath and another to inhale his scent. One hundred percent charge and here she blows.

The next thing she knew she was on her back and Xander was slapping her in the face lightly as a pool of his energy swirled inside her where hers was supposed to be.

"Abby, pull your energy back. I kept it in the room, just pull it back into you. Please, Abby, just do this."

"Okay." Relaxing into the nice supportive floor, she found all of her energy and put it back into her body until she was at fly-apart stage again. Xander's energy went back into him. He was a little pasty.

The jolt of his own energy hitting his body surprised him, but the color immediately returned to him. "Why did you do that?"

She sat up and propped herself on her hands. "I didn't need it anymore and I thought you may want it back."

"A better question for you. How did you do that?"

"No idea. I pushed it out of me, wadded it into a ball and shoved it at you. Your body seemed happy to have it back. Did I die?" She finally put two and two together. He had had to give her something to keep her alive because she had blown hers around the room. Stupid. Like a bad insulation job.

"Almost. You became drained. For a Nexus, that is pretty close." He was sitting back, kneeling and fighting the urge to do something...

She had no idea what. Kiss her? Kill her? Throw her back onto the floor and have his way with her? Nah. He was still in instructor mode.

"We need to keep you healthy and in control of your powers. I should have started with core training."

"Pilates?" She sounded hopeful, even to her own ears.

"No, but you may wish it was." He stood and began to lecture her on the methods of protecting core energy. The energy that her body needed to keep at all times.

He ran her through seventeen exercises and finally had to resort to charades to get the point across.

He held up two fingers in front of her. "This is your core energy. It swirls around you at all times, even when your talent is at rest. Can you identify that power?"

Sulking, she nodded. She perked up at his next demonstration. He made a tube with the fingers of the other hand and lowered it around the two fingers. That was too suggestive and she burst out laughing.

"Quiet. I know how this looks. But you have to do this. You need to create a barrier between your core energy and your working energy. If you don't, the first time that you purge excess energy, you will die."

She sat through his description of the variety of ways that she could change her magic to incorporate a personal permanent barrier. Then it was test time. She had to concentrate, explode, pass out, concentrate, explode, pass out, and finally she didn't pass out in between. "Ta-da! I still have it in me and my energy is spattered in here like a Jackson Pollock painting."

"Congratulations! Now I know you won't die when we keep training."

She crossed her arms and glared at him. She was exhausted, hungry and really wanted a cup of coffee.

"Well, I think you have gone far enough today. Do you have any questions?"

She grinned from ear to ear. "As a matter of fact I do." She took a wrinkled piece of paper out of her pocket and read off her question. "Do angels and demons really exist in some form or is that all fiction?"

"Angels are ethereal beings that rarely directly involve themselves in the daily operations of our world. They are quite pretty, if a little taller than the stories say. The average angel runs close to seven and a half feet tall. Women can't resist them."

"What about the demons? If angels are real, then the demons have to be, don't they?"

He handed her a glass of water from a tray on the table near where he had been perched. "Demons are very real and are very active in the mystical circles. They regularly interbreed with other beings, humans or not, and have wicked but not necessarily evil personalities."

"The angels keep to themselves?"

"As far as we know. The few children born in the past were...unpredictable." He sipped at his own water. "They don't talk about them, but they were described as beautiful and terrible."

"Ah, the Nephilim of the Bible."

"Indeed. Any other questions?"

"No. I need to pace myself, don't you think?"

He helped her to her feet and she stretched. His eyes immediately found the tiny sliver of naked skin bared by the hiked sweatshirt. He didn't touch so she lowered her arms and headed for the front door.

"See you tomorrow, Teach." The bolt on the door had been drawn so she unlatched it. It snapped back into position and she began to guess that he had it magically booby trapped. A look with her tired inner eye showed her that his energy was in it. She simply moved his aside with some of her own and the lock snapped open. She turned the handle and was out the door in an instant. "Bye!"

Walking down his well-manicured lawn was relaxing, but what she really needed was a good coffee.

Montrose's Munchies called.

She had to answer.

Chapter Seventeen

Day two of training started better. Abby got out of bed on her own when her alarm rang, showered and was waiting with a thermos of hot tea in her hand when Xander knocked at the door.

"Greetings oh great and wonderful, Safety Warlock." He seemed taken aback by her mood. "If you are wondering about my chipper attitude, I have been up for two hours and have had breakfast, a shower and watched morning television."

"Excellent. Shall we then?" Xander took the thermos from her and escorted her gallantly to his home. "I will have to admit to a certain amount of disappointment to not seeing you in your towel again. You have a great ass by the way."

A wash of heat worked its way through her face. "That was very frank."

"I am attracted to you, but I am going to try and keep it in my pants until we get you trained."

"Why wait?"

"Because I have no idea what that much energy will do to me if you come while I am inside you. I would rather you didn't blow my balls off. Well, not with magic anyway."

She laughed all the way to the training room. Today she admired the thought that went into the arrangement of the room. The walls were bare and, using her new senses, she could find the barriers that ran under the drywall and kept energy contained. It was designed for someone like her to blast the hell out of. Well, she would try. "Okay. I am fully charged, coach. What are we doing today?" She sat in her spot and took up the lotus position again. This time with her tea near at hand.

"Today, I want you to learn to hold your power in your hand."

She would rather hold his…"What? It's all over me, all the time."

"I know. But I want you to focus it on one point in your hand and force the power to make a physical appearance." He took up his own position and showed her what he meant. He held out his hand and looked down at his palm.

Abby couldn't help but notice that his nails were neatly trimmed and his hands were large. Oh goody. She jumped in surprise when a ball of power flared in his palm. She stared as she could see it whether she looked with her inner eye or not. It threw light into the semi-dark room and the colors of his magic took her breath away.

"All right, Abby. It's your turn." He closed his hand and the lightshow winked out.

"Good. Fine." Her chest expanded as she took a deep breath and she couldn't help but notice that Xander's gaze followed her breasts. As an experiment, she inhaled deeply once again, only to watch a dark flush cross his cheekbones. Aha.

Play time was over, it was time for training. She wrapped up her core as he had taught her yesterday and viewed the energy coating her. It was quite pretty, flowing with the oil-on-water iridescence that she loved. Abby could not just blow apart the magic as she had done the day before. This necessitated peeling the magic off and wadding it into a ball. Tricky.

One hand would not contain her full charge. She extended both hands and focussed on them. Mentally, she skinned the magic off her body and into her hands. It formed a shapeless mass the size of a half-filled hefty bag. Time to make a ball.

This was the truly tricky part. She wrapped strands of energy around the mass and wound it up like a ball of yarn. Her hands remained steady, but her mind was spinning. Finally, after what seemed like hours, Abby was looking at a bright and shiny mass of power the size of a basketball. Glowing with pride, and not a little sweat, she looked over at Xander. "Look what I made!"

His mouth opened and closed in shock. "Holy shit." He stood and moved to watch her holding the giant wad of power. "Is that an exceptionally large bundle of energy for you?"

"No. It feels about average." She suddenly had a bad thought. "You aren't upset because mine is bigger than yours, are you?"

He looked at her and gave a sharp bark of laughter. "I will beg to differ on that point, but you do hold more energy than I do. Can you re-absorb it now?"

"I would rather have somewhere to put it, but since I have filled all the pearls that you have, I think I will have to try and wear it until I can get to the rock." Lifting the ball, she put it on her head and let the strands fall around her body. It fell back into place easily. "Okay. So I have balls. What is next?"

He grabbed her hands and lifted her to her feet. "Nothing more today. You have been at that for hours."

So the time she felt passing had been real. Neat. She had been so focussed on getting it right that time had ceased to be important. "All righty. Can I ask you another question?"

"Shoot."

"Elves. Legolas or those little guys who made shoes? Are they a dignified race or tiny pervs who work for clothing?"

Another bark of laughter. "Somewhere in between. They are a race that varies in height and attractiveness. The elves are a little snotty, but basically good hearted."

"Are they represented in the inhabitants of Oak Point Way?"

"Not directly, no. As a species, they decided that this was an event that did not benefit them in any direct manner."

"You said *not directly*. Does someone here have elven roots?"

"Yeah. I do. Three generations back."

"So you are a big fairy at heart?" It was too much. Giggles overwhelmed her and she slumped in the hallway on her way to the door. The giggles turned into whoops of laughter as Xander watched her get her amusement out with his arms crossed over his chest. "That explains the antiques."

"If you weren't covered with enough energy to blow this place sky high, I would turn you over my knee."

"As if I would let you."

"I outweigh you by about fifty pounds, Abby."

"I kick and I bite."

His grin broke through. "We will have to try that one day."

Chapter Eighteen

Coffee with Seesee was a comforting ritual, it went so well with the exertions of the morning. Each day she debriefed Seesee as to her activities and the gorgon gave her cheesecake and coffee. It was a fair trade.

The third day of training involved a bit of cargo. Abby had found the dollar store in town and had picked up bags and bags of glass beads. The kind of beads that you could use to create a flower arrangement with the beads in the bottom of the vase.

Pretty and functional. It was a perfectly innocuous way to charge an item and then have it in a portable format.

Xander had looked surprised when she started dumping the bags of beads in front of her meditation station, but as she gained and drained power into them, he got the hang of it.

Today was a day for multi-tasking. Xander had assigned her to constantly drain her charge while keeping up a conversation. So she was choosing to ask him about magical races that she hadn't yet gotten to. "Okay. Dwarves. Are they really devoted miners, obsessed with gold, silver and other metals? Or are they a short group of humans who were trying to buy their way into the magical community?"

"That is a good one. All the dwarves that I have met have been hundreds of years old so they must have been imbued with magic at some time in their history. They are genuinely obsessed with mining and a conversation with them is like a geological survey of any region that is the topic. They just seem to know."

"Are they grubby?"

"No, they dress in the finest of clothing for the events. Lots of jewels as well. They wanted to send a representative to the neighbourhood, but they don't do well in persistent sunlight."

"Gotcha. Although it is probably the open spaces more than anything else that freaks them out." She was picking up the glass beads and charging them, then flicking them into the charged pile. She had even started locking them against accidental activation. A trick she figured out on her own.

"Probably."

"Next question. The bogeyman. Is he real or just a way to keep people in bed?"

"Real. He is a phantasm. He floats around and feeds on fear. He wouldn't do any physical harm, but he likes to hang around scared kids."

"So pervy, but real. Creepy." She was through over one hundred beads. Going strong. "Now. About gnomes. How many have been mobile in recent times?"

"None. Yours are the first. According to legend, they are fiercely loyal and dedicated to their work. You are going to have the best looking yard in town if they have their way."

"Great. So I put a target on myself with that one."

"You did indeed. They are the only gnomes that have actually come to life in recorded history. Well, them and the rogue ones that are coming alive around town."

"Fantastic. Okay, onto another race." She thought for a moment, her hands working on autopilot. "Goblins."

"What about them? Are they real?"

"Yeah, that is what I am asking."

"Hell, yes they are real. Their wisdom comes with age and they rarely achieve it. A more unpleasant race you could not find." He shuddered, but kept a close eye on her processing of the beads. "They tend to pick mates based on maximum deformity and on violence of temper. It makes for charming children with very sharp teeth."

"Eww. Creepy."

"Indeed. A creepy species that is best left alone."

"Will do. Now what about fairies?" This had to be less creepy.

"Fairies are an interesting thing. They appeared once, near Cottington England and then only sporadically. We think that the designer of the creatures was one of the short lived Nexus' that we mentioned."

"So the idea is to get me trained and out in the public so that no one will try and put dibs on me."

"You have hit the nail on the head, Abby. The easiest way to protect you is to put you in plain sight. There will still be attacks, but that is why we are here. All the members of the neighbourhood have been sworn to protect you. When you travel, we go with you. It's part of our vow when we were selected to take this assignment."

"Nice. I hope that you never have to use that vow."

"As do I. An attack on you would be a sad day for the magical community."

"I like to think so, too." She gave him a bright smile. "I'm sure that everything will be fine. I am not exactly a threat to anyone."

"Let's hope you are right. All done?"

"Yup. Four hundred blobs of glass. All charged. Did I just do your Christmas shopping for you?" She watched him look over her pile.

"Abby, the charge doesn't seem to be coming out of these."

"Hold it in your hand and rub it gently. I set these ones not to go off in your hands. Like M&M's." She smiled brightly and watched as he successfully opened the charge on one of the beads.

The little jump that he gave made her twitch in return, but he smiled as he threw the spent bead aside. "That is a fantastic idea."

"What are you going to do with them?"

He looked stern. "I am giving a box to all representatives on the council. Then they can't complain about you."

"Who is complaining?"

"A few council members are worried about this whole episode being run by the seers."

"Why?"

"They were the ones who announced your activation and they chose all the people in the neighbourhood. My grandmother is one of the seers and several of the council members are accusing her of sending me for matchmaking purposes."

"Matchmaking with whom?" Seesee? Laura? Miranda?"

"You, you dolt. She told me when I was little that my match was a Nexus, and the moment I saw you, I knew it was true. We just have to get your powers under control before we can do anything about it."

Her heart was practically melting in her chest. He felt the same attraction that she felt and was just as eager to take it for a test drive. "Wow. So how am I doing, coach?"

"Only a few more days and we can start dating." He pulled her in close and, after he had settled her against him from hip to thigh, lowered his head for a leisurely kiss.

She tried to raise her arms to wrap around his head, but he held her arms to her sides and made sure that she knew he was in control. Well, up until she nipped his lip and moved her tongue into his mouth, then he groaned and shook while making the satisfied noises of a large jungle cat.

Abby moved her head away from a kiss that made her want to be locked in it for eternity. Her power level was rising far too quickly for her peace of mind. If she was dangerous to Xander, she was hitting the stop button now.

He didn't want to stop.

His lips chased hers for a moment until she surrendered again. With no other alternative, she brought her knee up fast and hard. "I told you, I kick and I bite." She watched his pain-filled features with a small amount of sympathy. "My charge was climbing to a dangerous level. I didn't want to blow any part of you to bits. I like your bits."

"No, you would rather smash them personally."

"If you want to be a big baby about it, sure. The personal touch is always better, don't you think?" She stomped out of his house, blasting the deadbolt apart like it wasn't even there.

Her gnomes were gathered on the lawn, to greet or console her, she wasn't certain. Either way, her little honour guard fell into step around her as she moved into her home, her haven. Abby immediately went to the hearth and poured her pent-up magic into her home.

Stupid men. He was the one who was refusing to do anything with her until she was under control and then he pushes her past that control and is upset when she enforces the stop button.

"You are right, I am an ass." Xander was leaning in the open door. He still wasn't quite able to stand upright. "You blew out my lock, you know."

"I know. Sorry. The power has to go somewhere." She shrugged.

"I noticed that. My door now talks to me. It thinks I was a jerk. Can you recall that magic?"

So she had animated his door by accident. Too bad. Nah. She couldn't leave him with a talking door. The one time her toilet had pinched her ass had been enough for her to pull the power in seconds.

"Fine. Give me a moment." With her new skills, she had the energy sitting in a ball in her hand in a matter of seconds. She tossed it in the air. "Want it?"

"I think you had better not. Put it somewhere safe."

With a casual gesture, she launched it onto the hearthstone.

"You are putting your energy into your home?"

"Yes. I intend to live and die here. The more energy I give it, the more it will be mine." She shrugged. It was her logic and she was sticking to it.

"But where are you getting the spark of life that you are giving to it?"

"You can feel that, can you?" She patted the couch next to her and he sat. "In case you hadn't guessed, the energy flows into me during a few things, anger, fear, amusement and arousal. It was the last one that caused the big surge. The arousal energy is also the one that brings things to life."

If his jaw could have dropped to the floor, it would have. "How long have you known?"

"Since Harbinger got up to play hide and seek. And the others getting moving shortly after. Your presence was the only connecting factor and I drew the obvious conclusion." The creatures in question were offering them some iced lemonade in festive glasses. Abby thanked them and Xander took the offered beverage, but didn't say a thing. "After all, I had met the others and nothing had happened. It was meeting you that revved my engine."

She was trying to keep it analytical, but knowing that the man who wouldn't meet her eyes was just as attracted to her as she was to him was enough to make her want to leap on him to ravish him. Just to see if the end of the world would happen. Or if he would pop with the extra energy.

Why did that thought fill her with so much satisfaction?

Chapter Nineteen

WITH THE TRIUMPH AND DISASTER OF THE DAY BEFORE RINGING IN her mind, Abby tried to find a happy medium. A steady schedule that would keep her focus.

It was harder to establish a routine than she imagined and the workout Xander gave her self-control, taxed her on both a magical and sensual level. It took all the energy she had to not tackle him to the floor and have her way with him as he demonstrated meditation techniques and breathing exercises. They had given up on slap and tickle after she dropped her power-generating arousal bombshell.

Her afternoons were spent eating sweets and gabbing with Seesee who was teaching her to pipe cream into éclairs. More got on her than in the éclairs, but it was all in good fun and no one would be eating anything that Abby touched anyway. More for her.

Abby's gnomes did all of her cooking and housework and were digging postholes for a deck expansion. It was like they had read her mind.

It was a comfortable routine until one day…

"Listen, you little rodents! I am getting out of here whether you like it or not. Now move!" The barricade of tiny bodies blocked the door. As one, they stubbornly refused to move. They were stacked in a pyramid and were looking at her with a sense of urgency. She contemplated leeching some of her power from them, but they were her babies and she didn't want to hurt them. Aside from their odd behaviour, the only thing wrong was that they weren't all there. One of them was not in the throng.

The only gnome missing was Bitsy. His conspicuous absence was answered by a knock on the door behind her wall of gnomes.

There was only one person it could be. "Come on in, Xander. If you can." With the grace of tumbling leaves, the pyramid of gnomes dissolved to allow him in. They formed a column of honour and watched the magus enter with hope and relief in their tiny eyes.

"What's wrong, Abby? Bitsy grabbed me out of the shower." Xander was only wearing a set of jeans, and by the way they clung to him, he hadn't had a chance to dry off. Bitsy must have seen him naked. Lucky little bugger.

The surge of power that rippled through her house made her aware of the effect his half-naked presence was having on her. With reluctance, she fought the arousal away, feeling the power subside with it. So it only took one half-naked man to make her lose her control. How embarrassing.

"I have no idea what got into them. Their vocabulary isn't developed enough for what they want to tell me. I think Harby just ate my car keys so it must have something to do with my car." She turned from introspective to hopeful. "Maybe my battery is dead?" The only other possibility was that her creatures were holding her prisoner and were keeping her under house arrest. Nah, that was too ridiculous. A tug on the leg of her jeans made her look down.

Bitsy spread his arms wide. "Boom."

She blinked in surprise and then looked up as Xander started to move to the door.

"Let me check out your car, all right?"

As soon as she nodded, he was out the door and she felt *something* around her vehicle. Sheer nausea followed at his announcement.

"It's a bomb. Under the driver's seat."

The floor rushed up to meet her ass as her knees gave way again. "Are you sure?" Of course he was sure. He was a whiz of a wizard.

"Of course I am sure." He looked indignant and delectable at the same time. "Would you like me to remove it?" He crossed his legs at the ankle as he leaned against her ready-to-explode station wagon.

"Yes, please." It never hurt to be polite. She made the most of her manners. "That would be most kind of you. Thank you."

All of her blood was pounding through her head as she watched him gesture and mutter. With her eyes open, she triggered her second sight and watched his magic ebb and flow. The colors were wild, blue, brown and a shimmering black. A lovely display of phantom colors as the explosive device was levitated out from under her car to hover in front of it. The instant that it hit the daylight, it began to explode. Xander couldn't contain it.

The bomb was small but deadly as a dome of power encapsulated it. The only problem for her was that it wasn't Xander's power that had wrapped around it. It was hers. A bright sphere of blue, purple and gold. Iridescent and beautiful, they swirled around the explosion and held it in physical and temporal stasis.

Her day was looking up.

Chapter Twenty

"Are you doing that? Holding the explosion?" Xander looked exhausted and relieved. He was lying on the grass where the first shockwave had knocked him when the bomb began its explosion. The multi-coloured bubble was still hovering in mid-air, pulsing gently as it froze the bomb in time and space. The time thing was surprising. Abby didn't even know that it was possible, but there it was, frozen at the moment of explosion, still blowing apart, but wrapped with energy. Freaky.

"I guess I am." She slowly lowered the bubble to the ground and then blinked in astonishment as her gnomes charged forward with high cries and grabbed the sphere. In a stampede of tiny feet, they moved around the house to the backyard, leaving the humans gaping after them in bemusement. "What do you think they are going to do with it?"

He got to his feet with a groan. "I have no idea, but if they take it far away, I am happy to have it gone. How long do you think you can hold that power bubble?"

"The power is now out of me. I can hold it forever as long as no one drains it." She took the hand he extended as he climbed the steps.

As he pulled her to her feet, their bodies collided and magic flared.

The colors of their magic clashed in an explosion of fire and light, Abby abandoned herself to it and let her power flow. She backed up, dragging Xander with her, and manoeuvred him into her house, all without breaking the lip lock that had them plastered against each other from chests to toes. Abby regretfully broke the kiss to murmur, "The door." Then returned to the heaven of his lips parting hers so that their breath mingled and power collided.

Another thought distracted her and she pulled away again, "Maybe we should put a chair up against it? The gnomes are nosey." This time his right hand came up to hold her mouth to his as his left hand controlled some of the power and slammed the door. The screech of a chair being dragged across the floor had her smiling against his lips while he took care of his next goal.

That goal appeared to be to divest her of her t-shirt and bra. He went after it like she was hiding the Caramilk secret between her breasts. How he got her shirt off without breaking his contact with her skin would remain one of her great mysteries, but as he trailed his mouth down her neck and she let her head drop back to allow him full access to her flesh, she was happy for a few things to remain unexplained.

Her bra stymied him. For about ninety seconds. Then the hooks released with a click and she had the inkling that he cheated. Power drizzled down her spine and her nipples hardened as he slid her bra down off her arms and onto the floor. Her skin prickled in delight as he trailed his fingers over her breasts and across her ribs.

This was wonderful and his attention to detail was truly commendable, but she wanted him inside her. Now. Her fingers tackled his belt buckle and he returned the favour by unsnapping and unzipping her jeans. He had more success than she did and he pushed his fingers into the opening, scooting the denim off her hips as his fingers searched out and found her center. A few short and rapid strokes and the end was upon her. She came in a rush of moisture and power. Her knees gave way and Xander finally got her attention. He groaned with desire and she drowsily looked up to face the lust in his eyes.

It was his turn.

Magic stripped them both in a second and then he was bearing her back to the couch. She fell back with her thighs parted and waited breathlessly as he rocked against her, the heat and moisture from his flesh searing hers. Through the mist of hormones and swirling energy, she had a thought, "Whoa! Condom, Xander."

A darker flush mantled his already tight skin and his jeans hit him in the side of the face as he summoned them. The ubiquitous condom in the wallet was produced and he rolled it on with economical movements. Dressed for battle, he retook the field.

Her body was waiting for him and, as he moved back between her thighs, she hooked an ankle around the small of his back. "Xander, I want you now." It was all the encouragement that he needed. A sharp thrust brought him into her halfway and she gasped in surprise at the feel of it. Okay, she was a bit out of practice.

"Are you all right?" He was frozen above her, half in, half out, his arms trembling with the urge to finish what he started.

"I am just out of practice, is all. Continue." She tried to encourage him with her hips, but he was having none of it.

"I think we need to switch this around a bit." He backed away from her and took her hand, pulling her upright. He walked over to the wingback chair along one wall and took his seat. He smiled and patted his thighs. "As fast or as slow as you want it."

His erection drew her like a lodestone. Moving deliberately, she climbed up and moved to position him at her entrance. As if in a dream, she lowered herself inch by inch until his breath was heaving in his chest and she was trembling with the urge to impale herself completely.

The decision was soon taken from her. After two whole minutes of her rising and falling at her leisure, he gripped her hips and surged into her, pounding upward in a beat as old as time. She hung on to the rock hard curves of his shoulders for balance as he thrust deeply over and over. Abby began to shake, an orgasm the likes of which she had never felt before building within her.

And then he stopped. The bastard stopped.

Abby glared at him, she hoped that one tenth of the fury she felt was in her eyes.

He merely laughed at her and said, "Hang on."

He rose to his feet, wearing her. He held her hips to his as he crossed the room and laid her on her coffee table. She was draped across it like an offering and he was in the mood to worship. He draped her legs over his shoulders and drove into her one last time. This time he hammered into her with the express purpose of achieving an orgasm for herself and for him.

His fingers brushed the nub of sensation between them as he rocked and thrust into her. With all the previous stimulation, it didn't take her long before she was panting on the edge of release once again. As she gasped and shuddered with each impact, she noted the flaring lights in the room.

Something was going to blow, and with relief, it was finally her. No scream, no gasp and no howl made it through her throat, but the magic that blasted loose, shook the very foundations of her house. Xander's eyes widened as he was dragged along in her magical wake and his own orgasm shook him in its grip.

So much for first dates and self-control.

Chapter Twenty-One

WAKING FROM A POST-COITAL SNUGGLE TO FIND AN AUDIENCE of gnomes facing you would have disturbed a lesser being, but having gotten what she was after, Abby was made of sterner stuff. Barely.

Xander, on the other hand, jerked in surprise and threw the afghan from the back of the sofa over their bodies. "When did they get here?"

"I have no idea. But they seemed to have missed the big show." She tucked the blanket under her arms and levered herself upward.

"How can you tell?"

"They look neither shocked nor impressed." She turned to give him a quick peck and it turned into a considerably longer one. Until a small and curious hand started to grope her ass, that is. "Knock it off, Harby."

Sitting up, while ignoring Xander's newest arousal was a hard thing to do, no pun intended. "Guys. Shoo! Go do some dishes or reorganize the lawn. Sort the grass or something."

"Do they actually do what you tell them to?" He caressed her hips and drew her against him as her tiny army filed out of the room. Mitsy and Ruffles dragged Harby between them.

"Not usually, no. They just do what they want." She looked around on the floor and located her shirt and jeans. His hands were warm and the ridge of flesh that was pressing against her tailbone was hot. She was saved from another marathon session by the unmistakable ring of a cell phone emanating from the heap of denim that had landed by the fireplace. "Uh, Xander. Your phone is ringing."

"They can wait."

He burrowed his lips into the hollow of her throat and she

marvelled that he could almost wrap completely around her and reach every portion of her body at will. She let out a deep sigh and relaxed against him, loving the rise and fall of his chest under hers. It was only when a second round of breathing occurred that she had a sneaking suspicion that her magic had found some outlets.

She held her breath and waited. A sudden heaving of the couch beneath them had her cursing and leaping to her feet. "Xander. The couch is alive."

He lay flat, watching her nude body moving around the room, gathering her clothing right up until the moment when a velour tongue lapped at him from behind. At which point, he literally flew off the couch and landed across the room. "What the hell?"

Her panties and bra were missing, but her jeans went on without too much trouble. The rough denim chafed at the inside of her thighs slightly, but she did them up with a sharp inhalation and the relief that she was no longer vulnerable. Her t-shirt made the obvious protrusions of her nipples stand out, but until she could get fully dressed, it was better than nothing. The odd vulnerability that followed sex apparently did not get easier with age.

"Abby, why is the couch breathing?" He was back in his denim and looking at the rest of the furniture with trepidation.

"All that magic I was generating had to go somewhere." She wasn't completely honest. It had felt good to simply let go and let the energy flow. If she could claim ignorance on this one, she was going to. "You were no slouch, yourself."

"Can you still recall it?"

"Sure." She took deep breath and sought out all the energy with her signature in the area. The gnomes were in the backyard so they were safe as she drew the power back into her. It was quite a bit of stuff to contain, and it was only when she had it all in her that she realized that she had not thought of where she was going to put it.

Uh-oh.

With a sense of desperation, she walked past Xander and knelt directly before her fireplace. She laid her hands on the stones and started to dump power into them. It took a while. The stone resisted her energy when she started, but soon was absorbing it wholeheartedly.

"I don't know if you should be doing that inside your home. It could have unforeseen consequences."

"As opposed to the foreseen kind? Puh-leese." She was still giddy from their encounter and was not looking forward to coming down off the endorphin high. "My house, my magic, my business."

"Fair enough. But don't say that I didn't warn you."

"You are just crabby because the couch tasted your butt."

"That is not true, but it didn't help." His eyes gleamed in amusement. "We need to discuss a more important matter than my butt."

"The mind boggles. And what exactly is that?"

"Whom do you think just tried to blow you up?"

If ever there was a sentence designed to stop all light-hearted conversation, that was it. With her charge dispersed, she returned to the couch and sat heavily while the enormity of the events, which preceded their coupling sank in.

"Who would want to blow me up? Even before I was a Nexus, I rarely went out and pissed people off." Well, there had been a few parking incidences, but nothing recent.

He came over to comfort her and wrapped his arm around her shoulders. "I do hate to tell you this, but as a Nexus there will be people who will want to cease your existence. Others will want to control you and some will wish to use you until you are powerless."

Her head was in her hands now and she was in the pre-vomit position. "That is fantastic."

He rubbed her back to calm her. "There are also those like your neighbours on Oak Point Way who love the new magic that you are bringing to our world. We are here to defend and protect you. Even when you don't want us to."

She just wallowed in self-pity for a few moments. The hand on her back was nice, but she needed more. Squirming into the curve of his arm, she snuggled against him for the comfort that his heat brought her.

It begged one thought out of her. "What happens to your power when we, uh... Well, when your energy leaves your body?"

"I control it and bring it back to my body after the exertion is done."

Humph. She squinted at his arm under her hand and across her ribs and smirked. He had taken quite a bit of her power with him. The soft smile in her tone belied the seriousness of her next question. "How nervous do we need to be about the attempt to explode me?"

"I am calling a neighbourhood meeting at your house this evening to discuss it. You had best lay in some snacks and beverages." A quick kiss on her nose and the shirtless warlock was on his way out of her house.

"Stay home and keep safe, Abby. We need you alive, and I want your body. Again." A wink for goodbye and he was out the door.

Abby was alone.

Her gnomes were outside, probably with her missing underwear, and getting up to who knows what. She had just had some of the best and certainly the most athletic sex of her life and her partner had just swanned out of her house, none the wiser.

Someone wanted her blown to bits, and if it hadn't been for her little creations, she would have been. Three cheers for the gnomes.

Now it was time for serious business. A shower, a change of clothing and a set of comfy walking sneakers and she was ready.

THE PHONE CALL THAT had occurred while he was with Abby was one he had been dreading. The instant that he got into his home, the phone rang again. He picked it up and answered with, "Hello Councilman. What can I do for you?"

"You can tell me why there was suddenly a pulse of magic that emanated from your location and continued outward?"

"The Nexus lost control for a few moments, Councilman."

"Have you learned her triggers?"

The spot behind her neck, the skin under her breast, the inches between her belly button and her sex. "I have identified a few of them, Councilman."

"When will you have your report ready? We need to know what we need to keep the Nexus happy."

"She seems to be embracing the environment that we have been creating and it seems to be stimulating her creative and energy producing urges. Oak Point is definitely the right place for her at the right time."

"It is good to hear. But please find a way to confine her emanations. They are setting off chain reactions across Canada and the United States. Garden ornaments are exhibiting a certain mobility that they have not before."

"Sir, before we conclude, there was an attempt on Abby's life today. Someone planted a car bomb in her vehicle."

The cursing on the other end of the line was indistinct, but heartfelt, "What was the result?"

Abby and I got naked and writhed around on every piece of furniture in her living room. "The bomb was removed and the explosion contained. The perpetrator has yet to be located." It was probably best to stick to the basics.

"Find them. We only have one chance at a Nexus during this generation and I don't want her to die before the power she can bring is shared."

Of course the power would be the major concern. Abby's life meant nothing to them without the potential magic she could produce. "We are attempting to locate the assassin and will, of course, bring them to the Council for sentencing when they are caught."

"Excellent. Now keep the Nexus under control. I don't need my yard flamingo talking to me." The councillor hung up the phone and Xander was left with a simmering anger.

He wanted to find the person who had tried to attack Abby and take them apart with his own hands. To hell with magic, he wanted to go medieval on their ass.

Abby was rapidly becoming a precious addition to his life.

Chapter Twenty-Two

Freshly showered, teeth brushed and in a fresh set of underwear under her jeans and the t-shirt that she has been wearing earlier, she was ready for a change of venue. The gnomes were nowhere to be found and therefore her car keys were still AWOL. "I guess I am walking."

There was no one to hear her, but she felt perversely better for speaking into the silence. The air in the house had changed, it now felt friendlier. It had always been cozy, but now she was convinced that this was where she belonged. It felt good to be home at last.

On that note, she steeled herself and left the warm and comfy nest that she had created and headed out to score some chocolate. Abby warily moved around her once-beloved car, not sure how to feel about it now that it had almost become the instrument of her demise.

Her sneakers made a light thumping noise on the pavement. It echoed around the cul-de-sac of Oak Point Way. She passed Laura's stately home, then Randy's tidy yard and Seesee's funky and multi-coloured front door. The house on the end must host the fabled Miklos. The guy Seesee was crushing on.

Based on what she already knew about the inhabitants of the Way, she wasn't sure that she wanted to meet him. Just the way that Seesee talked about him made her shiver.

The walk was refreshing, the cool breeze lifting and frolicking with her still-damp hair and the path to the center of town led her clearly into Sargent. The countryside surrounding the small town was unspoiled. Brooks babbled, trees rustled and the path next to the main road was tidy and well maintained.

It was the perfect environment for Abby to calm herself after the near death experience that morning. She wondered idly how Seesee would take the events of Abby's morning?

Seven minutes of peaceful walk later, she found out.

Apparently, *How many Nexus' does it take to defuse a car bomb in her front yard?* was not a good way to break the ice.

Upon hearing the flippant question and viewing the seriousness in Abby's eyes, Seesee's hair almost lost control. Her entire coiffure seemed to grow larger for an instant before it calmed and resumed its previous dimension.

When she had calmed herself, and her hair, Seesee felt she needed to ask, "Are you all right? Were you hurt?" Her gaze assessed every inch of Abby that was visible to the eye.

"No, just kind of stunned. Xander was there and he helped to remove it from my car." She stopped her conversation there and waited for the latte that she had ordered when she came in.

The beverage was delivered by a smiling server and Seesee held her patience no more. "Abby, tell me everything."

"Well, I wasn't much of a student in school, mostly Bs and Cs. It was only when I took clay and sculpture in art class that I found my true calling." She paused for a sip of the latte. Mmm...lovely.

"That is not what I was talking about Abby. Tell me about this morning. I felt the magic pulse, what caused it?"

"The long story or the short one?"

"The long one."

"Goody. There isn't a short one. This morning I had my usual tutorial with Xander, then showered, then got ready to come here for a visit. The gnomes wouldn't let me leave. They had barricaded the door and all other entries or exits had been nailed shut. A pyramid of growling gnomes stood between me and my car and when Harby swallowed my car keys, I knew I wasn't going anywhere."

"Bitsy had run out while I was in the shower to fetch Xander and he arrived at the door as I was contemplating gnome bowling. As soon as he arrived, the pyramid dispersed, little buggers. Bitsy came up to me and said *boom*, then ran with the others to watch Xander levitate the bomb."

"It must have had a solar trigger, because as soon as it came out from under the car, it blew." Abby shuddered in remembrance. "It was only after the shock of the explosion wore off that we saw that the explosion had been frozen in time and space. In a power ball of my own making. That was a shocker."

"Really? Your power held it?" Admiration filled her face. Apparently Abby's feat was a little tricky.

"Is still holding it. Will hold it until the power is diverted somewhere else I suppose." She shrugged.

"Really? So that was the power wave that happened? The bomb?"

"Uh, no. To be honest, the power wave came later. I had an uncontrolled moment and that was the side effect." She hoped her blush would be explanation enough. Apparently it was. Naked details were best left between her and Xander. And of course, the gnomes. Little perverts.

Seesee expressed the shock that was still reverberating within Abby, "Who would want to kill you?"

"You have got me. I don't really go around ticking people off and I don't date much so it must be a Nexus related vendetta."

"What does Xander think?"

"He said he was going to look into it."

"I should hope so." Seesee's lips twitched. She was not hiding her amusement well at all.

"Well, it isn't like a Nexus is born into modern society every day. Perhaps someone feels that magic has had its time." The philosophical approach seemed the best one to take. The adage of *tough tacos* would not be appropriate to the mood.

"The world would be a sad place without magic in it."

"I don't know about that. I managed just fine without magic for most of my life."

Seesee looked surprised "But, Abby, whether you knew it or not, magic was always with you. It was inside you and waiting."

"Okay, now that is just getting creepy." The thought of something nesting inside her and waiting for its moment made her shiver.

"Nevertheless, you have always been the Nexus, the gateway through which magic would flow. Speaking of which, what did manage to make you lose control enough to loose that pulse earlier? It was quite the blast of energy."

Damn, now they were back on that track. "It was a residual charge that I dissipated after the bomb. There was just so much energy and I suppose I am still a little sloppy when it comes to controlling the power."

Thankfully, Seesee seemed to accept that answer. "Well, sure. That makes sense. I say, all that time you are spending training with Xander is really paying off if that is the result."

Her mind skittered down a whole other path before she could stop it. Finally she realized what Seesee was referring to. "What? Oh. Yeah. The lessons in self-control are working just fine. I suppose." She remembered their other topic. "I mean, aside from that accidental burst."

"I have to say that I am impressed. You have hugged me every time you have seen me this week and no power has transferred. You are doing very well, Abby." The gorgon was all support and warmth.

Abby was blushing at the praise. She could feel the heat in her cheeks. "Yeah, you are right. And my toilet seat has only bitten my ass once. I may be getting good at this magic stuff."

"Self-control is never wasted."

On that note, Abby finished her complicated coffee, hugged Seesee goodbye and returned to the path back to Oak Point Way.

She was lost in thoughts about magic, gnomes and a naked Xander. Traffic passed her by and birds chirped in the trees with squirrels cursing at them. It was all terribly bucolic until she vaguely registered the sound of a car moving off the road and onto the shoulder. Fast.

When it didn't slow, she turned to confront the car while backing off the path in case the vehicle could not stop. Adrenaline pounded through her as the car inexorably approached her, her nerves burned and flared as the grill of the vehicle took up all of her attention. Impact was a bitch.

Abby flew through the air with her hands out in front of her. It had been the final gesture of defence before her magic had kicked in. She skidded to a halt on her back when the momentum of impact fetched her up against a pine tree. Sparks of energy danced in front of her eyes as she blinked to clear her vision. Bolts of pain replaced it.

"Ow. Son-of-a-fucking-bitch." Shaking like a leaf, she crawled out from under the pine to rise to her feet. The car that had almost killed her was long gone, the tracks that it had left behind chilled her. The driver had sped up to hit her. The gouges on the turf and across the walking path were brutal proof of murderous intention. That was it, Abby lost her latte.

Someone was really trying to kill her. Really. And they were in one fucking hurry.

Oops, there went the rest of the coffee.

As she limped back to Montrose's Munchies, she mulled over the event in every detail. She had been walking, then she heard the car, then turned to look at it, but no matter how hard she tried, she couldn't remember the damned license plate number. It had a plate, she was sure of that, but she couldn't read it. It was fuzzy for some reason.

The car itself also kept slipping through her memory. Now that she actually knew magic was real, she suspected that it had something to do with her faulty memory.

She had reached out with her hands to stop the car and a bubble of magic had formed around her. The car had not bounced so much as slid off her. The pressure of the compressed magic had thrown her backward and, based on the looks that passersby were giving her, she looked like she had been writhing in the mud and leaflitter.

Abby pulled open the door to Seesee's emporium and was gratified to see the gorgon's eyes widen when she got a look at her. The phone leapt into her hand and she was calling the neighbours in a second. Abby took a seat and waited.

A coffee appeared near her hand and, in light of her recent disgorgement, it was not at all appealing.

"Drink it. It will steady your nerves." Seesee's hand was on her shoulder.

When Abby looked up, she was astonished at the concern in her face. It was more than just the concern for the Nexus, it was concern for Abby. "Can I get green tea with four sugars instead? My last coffee is decorating the forest floor." Her friend nodded and gave the order to the barista manning the counter. Her hands were being held in a warm soothing grip and she realized that her body was ice cold.

"Abby, what happened?"

The sympathy almost moved her to tears. She took a deep and shaking breath. "Walk. Car. Bubble. Bang. Ouch. Here." Her earlier eloquence escaped her as it kept sinking in. Someone was trying to kill her.

The sweet tea was refreshing and she noted that there was a hint of lemon. A smile spread over her as heat and warmth sank back into her body and soul. A cool tugging at her hand made her aware of the first aid that Seesee was applying to her hand and she traded her tea from left to right as each hand was treated in turn. The blood on her hands hadn't sunk into her consciousness. It was just as well she had gone to Seesee for help. She was obviously in no shape to help herself.

They sat in silence, Abby drinking tea and remembering to breathe and the gorgon tending to her wounds.

Finally, as if years had passed Abby watched Xander walk through the door, the rest of the neighbourhood behind him. The cheerful tinkling of the bells was a counterpoint to the pure hell in his eyes. For some reason, she felt lighter and smiled as his scowling countenance drew closer. He was here. As he reached out to hug her, the embrace was fierce and tender at the same time. No power on earth could separate them at that moment.

As the rest of the Oak Point Way inhabitants drew around them, she realized that all of the regular patrons had left the shop. The two remaining employees were closing up for the day. In mere minutes, they were all alone. A deep rumble in her ear took her a while to decipher.

"Are you all right? Are you hurt?"

Suddenly, the urge to soothe him took over. "I am fine. A little scuffed and really dirty, but fine." She laid a small kiss on the hollow of his throat, feeling it work against her lips with the pounding of his heart. "I survived it, Xander, now let's find the bastard who is trying to kill me."

Silent and solemn, the others followed them out of the shop, falling into a guard around them. Verne led the way in his vehicle, then Xander and Abby, Randy, Laura and Seesee. It was a direct procession back home and an even more grim parade when they stopped and entered Abby's home.

It was time for a battle plan and Abby was more than ready for a fight.

Chapter Twenty-Three

TAKING CHARGE THE INSTANT THAT THEY CROSSED HER THRESHOLD, Abby began barking orders, "Boys, girls, please ask the gnomes for coffee or tea. I am going to grab a shower before I deal with anything else." Xander started after her as she moved down the hall. "Alone." When she was sure that no one was following her, she continued to her bedroom. Home. She could breathe again.

She was selecting her underwear when Bitsy peeked out from beneath her bed. A long look at his earnest face and she finally sighed. "Dude, it is nice that you care, but you are not following me into the shower."

As his little face became upset, she recanted, slightly. "Find one of the girls to keep an eye on me if you must."

He held his little hands out in the stay-put sign said, "Wait." Then he skittered down the hallway.

Wow. So she hadn't imagined it when he had warned her of the *boom*.

Mitsy followed Bitsy down the hall and stopped at the door to the bathroom, waiting for her to gather her things and come over for her shower. It looked like Abby's babysitter was on duty.

Bitsy took up a position at her bedroom and, as she listened closely, she could hear the gnomes puttering in the kitchen. She was safe here.

A cordial nod to both gnomes as she passed them was returned. Mitsy closed the door once she was inside the bathroom with Abby. It was her quickest shower ever. Dirt and leaves rained into the drain, her soap turned grey as she frantically scrubbed and she peeled off the dressings that Seesee had placed on her hands. Nothing on her body but water was what she was after and what she got.

Finally, the water ran clear, her tears melted into the water. Self-pity was destructive, but she couldn't help but wallow in it for a moment. Everything was new, foreign, strange. Someone wanted her dead and she didn't know why.

She dried her tears with a towel and shut the water off. She needed to get back to the group. They were going to try planning her safety and she had no idea what that would entail, but she could be sure that she wouldn't like it.

"Who is after her?"

"Are there any traces?"

"Have there been threats?"

"What does the council think?"

The last question Xander could answer. "The council doesn't know about this last attack yet. I haven't told them." Two of Abby's creatures were in the kitchen preparing coffee and putting the kettle on. Another was creating some sort of canapé platter.

He looked down the hallway toward the bathroom where the shower was singing its song. Abby was wet, soapy and naked in there and he was stuck trying to find out who was trying to take her from him before he could explore the depth of his feelings for her.

It was enough to fill any magus with rage.

With her creatures around her, he could be sure that she was kept safe. It was too bad that she couldn't remain alone at home. Whoever was doing this knew her routine.

The other inhabitants of Oak Point Way were scattered across a variety of furnishings. Laura was so upset that she gripped Verne's hand as he sat next to her on the loveseat. They were all looking to him for a solution and Xander only had the first step.

"I am making the call." He flipped his phone open and seconds later, he was connected to the head of the council. The same man that had assigned them all here, Bertrand Armgart. Bertie if you were female.

"What is it, Xander?" Bertrand sounded irritated and the high-pitched whisper in the background gave some reason for his mood. He was being interrupted. "Is the Nexus out of control? Do you need to bring her in?"

"No, sir. There was a second attempt on her life today. I felt that the council should be aware of it." He steeled himself for the blast. It wasn't long in coming.

"What? Is she all right? Is she safe? Has her power been damaged? Where are you calling from?" The barrage kept coming and Xander held the phone away from his ear while the councillor ranted.

"We are all in Abby's home, the entire neighbourhood, with the exception of the vampire contingent. He is still out of town."

"What are you doing about it?"

"There will be a watch kept on Abby around the clock until the stalker is found."

"Good, keep me posted." There was a pause from the councilor. "Were the attacks magical in nature?"

"No. Nothing in the first attack that I could detect. I have not had time to investigate the second one. It happened less than an hour ago. The first was a car bomb. The second has not yet been discussed."

Seesee piped up, "A car hit her. It was a hit and run."

Xander returned to the call. "It was a hit and run. She was hit by a vehicle."

"Damn. Keep her safe, Xander. At any cost to yourself or the others. We can't replace her." The line went dead.

Xander closed his phone slowly. He knew why the councillor was disappointed. Magic could be traced easily, a vehicular assault couldn't.

"There was a bomb?" Miranda expressed what the others were thinking. Well, everyone except Seesee who had obviously been told by Abby earlier.

"Someone is trying to kill Abby. They planted a car bomb between last night and this morning, if not for her gnomes, she would be dead by now." Xander gave the little ones the credit that they were due. If Bitsy hadn't come to get him, he shuddered at what would have happened.

The shock that was pulsing in the room was almost palpable.

Miranda pitched in, "We all know that a new Nexus was not a universally welcomed addition to our community. Add the fact that she was an outsider to our community and you have a giant target on her. Everything makes her situation worse."

Verne nodded in agreement. "My own pack discussed sending a representative, even after I volunteered. They hold contempt for human magic and could not see the benefit in having a new Nexus. Short-sighted idiots."

Mitsy brought in a tray full of mugs and Xander stared. If Mitsy was here then Abby was...

"So a portion of the magical community thinks that I am a waste of space? Why am I not surprised?" Wearing a blue sundress that draped like a toga, she took up her place in the empty wingback chair that he had such fond memories of. God, had it been just this afternoon? Even after all she had been through, she sat before them like a queen. And he had to lean forward to hide his erection.

From her throne, she took control of the meeting as if she were the most experienced magus, creature or supernatural being in the room. "So your theory is that someone in the community is trying to bump me off?"

Her voice reflected a change in her bearing—she was harder, stronger than she had been just an hour ago. Her evolution was astonishing. And lord, he wanted to get her naked again. "The magical community. Not ours. And yes, that is the theory."

"Fantastic." The gnomes had distributed the beverages and laid out the canapés, now they took positions around her chair. "So what exactly is our next move?"

What followed was a discussion that made Xander's head spin. It took several hours and rounds of coffee, three snack trays and four dozen cookies. The gnomes were excellent bakers.

"OKAY, WE ARE ALL in agreement. I will rotate my residency with each of you. Even you won't know where I will show up next because I will draw names from a hat before I come over." Abby's voice was giving out. "Please let me know now whose home I need to bring pillows and blankets to."

In the end, the only truly safe person for Abby to be with was herself. But her home was obviously not safe. The stalker was familiar with her and her vehicle so she was stuck staying with a new member of her neighbourhood every day. Random draw was the only way to make sure that they didn't know whose house she would be off to next. Even a mind reader would not be able to figure out where she was going if she didn't know.

"So all direct contact with me is cut off and your only go betweens will be the gnomes. They have agreed and they know where I am the whole time anyway." She outlined the complicated procedure. "You will leave a tennis ball with a message tied to it in the courtyard. T he gnomes will retrieve it and bring it to me."

She sighed in frustration at the lengths they had devised to keep her safe. She had wanted to make up a schedule, with Xander's name at the top, and every other day, but had been vetoed by the others. They wanted her safe, at all costs. Even that of taking in a houseguest with no notice.

Miranda stated, "Even their own group could be leaking information." At those words, a plan was devised to keep her segregated from the group at large at all times. Bummer.

If the stalker was by some weird stretch of the imagination, one of their group, then Abby would be walking into their home defenceless, but no one listened to her logic. It was as if they didn't hear her and just kept on with their plans.

She trusted all of the inhabitants of the neighbourhood, with her life even. Which was a good thing as that was exactly what this meeting was about. She was about to place her safety in their hands. And they would never know when. Lovely.

Chapter Twenty-Four

ARMED WITH HER SLEEPING BAG, BACKPACK, PILLOW UNDER ONE arm and a guard of garden gnomes , she stomped up the steps of her first victim. With a deep breath, she reached out and rang the bell. A ship's klaxon rang in the house.

As the door creaked, open she chirped, "Laura, you are today's winner or loser, depending on your point of view." A thermos of coffee banged against the doorframe as Laura waved her inside. The mermaid didn't drink coffee so Abby brought her own.

A close look at her host had Abby groaning. Laura's hair was perfect, her complexion was perfect and she was obviously a morning person. Ugh.

"Come on in, Abby. The guest room is ready to go. You didn't need to bring your sleeping bag." She led the way through halls that gleamed in a pearlescent manner. Over each door was an embossed shield featuring a mermaid.

Abby examined one closely. "This is beautiful. Is it you?" It looked a lot like Laura. Even the jawline was hers.

Her host stopped for a moment and looked at where she was pointing. "Thank you, but no. That is my great-grandmother, Sorwiniven. She fell in love with a sailor who broke her heart, then ended up in the arms of my grandfather. He was a sculptor and madly in love with her."

"Well, it ended well for her." She mulled over the tale. "Did the sailor reject her because she was a mermaid?" Maybe all the fairy tales were true. Or maybe not.

"Nope. In fact he fell in love with another of the sea folk while he was with her. One with bigger tits."

Abby was sure her jaw was unhinged. She closed her mouth with some difficulty. Giggles welled up within her. "Men. Give them a mermaid and they still can't commit. Gonads rule the roost."

Chuckling, Laura continued to lead her to the guest room. Chamber actually. This was no simple room. A gracious four-poster encrusted with pearls, gold and silks. "This is amazing, thank you again. I am sorry to impose."

Laura gave her a short hug. "I should be thanking you. That power blast that you gave me really had me rethinking my life on land, or in the ocean."

"Being trapped in a swimming pool will do that for you."

She gave a short laugh, "I guess. Come on, I have a light snack ready."

"I just hope that you don't mind the gnomes running around, they are erring on the side of the overprotective." As the words left her mouth, a clattering came from the kitchen. "And the warning comes not a moment too soon."

Laura led the way to the site of the noise and she laughed at the sight of Skint and Ruffles arranging scaffolding for them to reach the counter. Splint was holding a chair in position while the others were working to build a sturdy set of steps.

"Okay. Sorry. It is no longer your kitchen. Land of the gnomes is firmly taking over." Abby was hovering in the doorway as she watched her creatures move around the new territory and Laura's reaction to it. "I think that they will bring us some lemonade and the snacks if we go outside. Would you care to?"

"Wow. They are really making themselves at home, aren't they?" Laura was slightly stunned.

Abby tugged her into the backyard through the patio doors. She sat her host across from her on the shaded lounges and they waited for the small servers. "So do you have any brothers or sisters?" It seemed like a good way to make small talk.

"Three sisters and four brothers." Laura's face lit up slightly. "My grandmother is still alive. She's the one who told me the story of

Sorwiniven and the faithless sailor."

"Can I ask you some mermaid questions?"

"Sure. Can I ask you some Nexus questions?" Laura's eyes were twinkling now. Skint delivered some glasses and Mitsy followed with the lemonade. Inside, it appeared that Harby was working on the counter, putting something on a platter.

"I don't know if I can answer them, but sure, give them a shot." She took a sip of icy lemonade and grinned. "I get to go first."

"Fine."

"Can you have sex while you have the tail?" She leaned to the side to avoid the spray of sweet and sticky fluid that emanated from Laura.

"That was direct."

"Thank you. What is the answer?"

"Uh, it is easier with another merperson, but it is possible with someone with legs. We just have to make some adjustments. Of a scaled trap door variety."

"Neat. And kinda cool, but also weird."

"My turn. Where does the power come from? Does it come from you, do you have to summon it?" Laura was slurring slightly. A light touch of the aspirated lemonade left on the table and a sniff was all Abby needed to know. Laura was hammered. The gnomes had doctored her glass. Protective little buggers.

"From what Xander has told me, and the few books he has let me read, I am a gateway between a dimension of magic and this world."

"But what lets the magic through?" She sloshed some lemonade on the table as she asked the question. She was going under fast.

"Hormones. That one even Xander doesn't know, but he might suspect." She watched as the mermaid slowly sank to the table to have a little nap. "Okey dokey. There goes all polite conversation. Perhaps I will just have a little snag of meditation then." She was talking to herself and the gnomes. Moving slowly, so as not to wake Laura, she wandered over to the side of the pool and sank to her knees.

The jets of the pool had a soothing rhythm. As she closed her eyes and gave herself up to the sound, she pulled magic in and let it flow again.

As Laura snored on, her sounds became part of Abby's magic, she synched her breathing to the drunk mermaid and her body relaxed enough to let her mind wander. So out of her body she went.

The oak tree greeted her spirit as it passed, the rock was indeed sitting on its root ball and her week of dumping magic into the stone had given the tree enough life to move and communicate with her on a basic level. She missed their *chats* and it had only been a day.

The town was as neat and tidy as always. Seesee was doing a brisk business, or at least her shop was. If she had stuck to the plan, she was at home to confuse the stalker.

The people of Oak Point Way probably knew where she was, but they wouldn't say anything. Unless they were the one who was out to kill her.

That one thought explained why the gnomes had dosed Laura. They didn't know if she was the stalker so they were taking no chances. Seesee was the only safe person because she had been at work when the car had tried to take Abby out. Or so she thought. In theory, Seesee could have gotten into her car, charged at Abby and then returned to her shop with no one the wiser. That thought unsettled her to the point where she shook herself back into her body.

Her hands were numb, her legs asleep and she wasn't even sure if her feet were still attached. With a groan, she rolled herself onto her hip and used force to straighten her limbs.

An answering groan sounded from the deck and Abby looked over to see Laura moving sluggishly at the table, sitting up and clutching her head. "Hey, scooter, you might want to take it easy. You got hammered."

Laura winced at the noise of Abby's voice, but moved slowly regardless. "You drugged me?"

"No. I didn't. The gnomes did. I am guessing that they were giving me some quiet time. And plenty of it." The sun was already beginning to set. The day had been lost in a haze of magic and reflection. Abby crinkled her nose. She was sunburned. And hungry. Really hungry.

On cue, her tiny keepers marched out with a fully prepared dinner. Their timing was almost…magical. Oh, heck. The tingling was starting.

Laura was there the instant that Abby groaned.

"Abby, what is it? Why aren't you moving?" The mermaid was hovering.

"I meditated in the wrong position and the wrong jeans. My legs and feet are asleep." She breathed shallowly, desperate to not move her body. "Give me a minute. Or six."

"Forgive me for this, Abby." Laura picked her up and dropped her in the pool.

The shrieking and cursing was conveyed mostly in bubbles underwater, frightening the few fish that still occupied the pool. They swam in to get a look at her and she flailed her arms and pounded her fists on the floor of the pool. But hey, her legs felt better.

Sighing, she stood, happy to have been thrown in to the shallow end. Her legs held her weight as she stood and glared at Laura. The mermaid was looking smug.

"You drug me and I dump you in a pool. We are even." She held out her hand and Abby took it. "Do your legs feel better?"

"Yeah, they do. Thanks." Water sluiced from her as she made it back to the edge of the pool and onto the wood of the nearby deck. "Your penalty is to have me soak all your furniture."

"I will accept it. But I have no idea what we were discussing."

The gnomes had cleaned up the table and set it for two. As Mitsy and Ruffles put plates and utensils down, Abby got another suspicion.

"We were talking about Nexus's and mermaids. And love lives. What is it with you and Verne?" Yep, the little buggers were plating her food and Laura's from separate pots. "And hey, would you humour this crazy Nexus and share food off my plate. I think it may be a good plan for dinner."

"You think they are going to…"

"Pretty sure. Do you want to chance it?"

"Not really." Laura flicked a napkin into her lap.

Abby did the same. "Is Laura your real name? Most mermaids that I have read about have slightly more fantastical names."

"Good call. I think only the boys and Miranda get to use their regular names in the modern world. Lorifinianalwen. That is the name my parents stuck me with."

"Wow. I got away with Annabeth. My middle name is a bit of a bitch, but it fits in the little boxes on government applications."

"What is it?"

"Bodicea. After an old English queen who went insane after herself and her family was abused by the Romans and tried to expunge them from the island. Permanently."

"What island?"

"Britain. Or I guess Britannia back then."

"That is one heckuva namesake. I was just named after an aunt who found a new source of food."

"Really? What?"

"Tacos. She was off the coast of Mexico and went up to a resort in the fifties. They were serving soft tacos and she took some back to the hub, turning herself into an instant hero. Because my mom was pregnant with me at the time, and scarfing every taco that Auntie could lay hands on, I was named after her."

"My mom just read a book. I was almost Anne Boleyn Hanover. That would have been creepy." She did some math in her head, "How old are you anyway?"

"Close to sixty. My birthday is in the winter."

"Did you volunteer to come here?"

"More or less. My family is the delegate to the council. We tend to pop onto land as requested." The shrug spoke volumes. Family honour came first.

"So how did the houses get assigned?"

"Well, all I know is that I was promised the one with the pool so here it is." Her hands took in the entire yard and house.

"Nice." And it was. She was guessing that the internal décor was all Laura though. The pearl and iconography gave it away.

Her own house suited her to a tee. She wondered idly as she waited at the table to partake of the gnomes' offerings, who had done the research on her before she had gotten here? "Well, regardless of how it was set up, your home is truly lovely. It suits you." She sat back as the gnomes trundled a service cart over and began to serve them from plated dishes. As a test, Abby reached out to pick up Laura's soup. "That looks lovely. Mine has too much broccoli in it. Do you mind if we switch?"

Laura looked a bit confused, but understanding crossed her features at last. "Certainly. I do love my green veges. I normally eat raw plankton while at sea." They exchanged plates and, as the gnomes had tiny coronaries, she smirked.

"I don't want you dosing my hosts. I know that the best way for me to be safe is to be alone in a home with the host unconscious, but it is just rude. I have to trust these people and they will have to trust me eventually. This isn't helping."

The small solemn faces nodded unhappily. They began to take the tainted dishes back to the kitchen.

"I also think that you all owe Laura an apology. So do I for that matter. Laura Exner, I am sorry for the actions of my gnomes. They acted in my best interest but are overzealous and only a few weeks old. Could you forgive me? And them?" Abby bent her head and waited.

"I accept your apology. Your creatures acted most honourably on your behalf. There is no need for forgiveness." She smiled and reached out to take Abby's hand in her cool one.

"Whew. Thanks for that. I just wanted to say it before they did something else to you, like throw you in the pool and put the cover on."

"A wise decision." She giggled. "There isn't a cover for my pool, by the way. So I am not worried."

The second undrugged, round of soup and salad arrived and they cautiously had Abby eat from both bowls and plates before continuing. *Better safe than stupid* was Abby's motto. That and, *Always know where your pants are.*

The rest of the evening was uneventful. They finished dinner and helped the gnomes do the dishes. Well, they tried to, the gnomes were exceedingly territorial.

They didn't share the same taste in movies so compromised by watching the food network. Hours flew by, popcorn was provided, eaten and removed and then it was time for bed.

"Goodnight, Laura. See you in the morning."

"Only if I get up before you head off to your next host."

"Oh, right. Bummer." She ran forward and hugged her host and let a little bit of energy seep from her hug, into Laura. "Just a little to say that your sacrifice of a day was appreciated. Not enough to make you all taily."

Tears were in Laura's eyes as they separated. "Just enough to make me the sturdiest damned mermaid in existence. The last time, my scales were like armour and my skin felt like steel. This time, I will be coated in power." A sudden thought occurred to her. "You are in control of it now, aren't you?"

"Shh...don't tell my stalker or they may try and wipe me out while I sleep."

"Three of your gnomes are outside keeping watch. I think you will be safe tonight." Laura turned and moved to her own room. "Goodnight, sleep tight. It has been fun having you here."

"For me, too. Good night." Abby was alone in her room at last.

Her guard was outside in the form of Harby and Bitsy, her two most devoted gnomes. The others must have been outside patrolling the neighbourhood. She was confident that they would be there when she needed them, if she needed them.

Now it was time for bed.

XANDER WAS IN HER DREAMS.

She didn't bother asking him what he was doing there, she simply jumped him and straddled him, willing his clothing away. He tried to ask her a few questions, but she silenced him. At his astonished look, she smiled. "My dream, my rules. Talk later."

She rubbed her body against him, revelling in the feel of the hair on his chest rasping against her. Huh, apparently, she was naked from the get go in erotic dreams. And she wanted this dream to get erotic, fast.

His erection had been a little sluggish, but under some gentle coaxing, he was soon surging into her hand. She twisted against him and eventually straddled him. His heat against the slick dampness of her entrance and then the blunt head slowly moving into her as she sank onto him with delicious attention to his frantic movements. He wanted her to ride him and she would. In her own time.

Rising and falling slowly with gradually increasing speed, propelled her headlong into the release that she had been seeking. "It's your turn, go nuts." *Her statement had only escaped her sated body by seconds when she was flipped over onto her belly, was drawn to her knees and he was thrusting into her with a passionate frenzy.*

When he was spent, he withdrew and fell to her side. "Now can we talk?"

"It's your nickel so talk."

"So Laura is not the one?"

"The stalker? No. The gnomes are starting to qualify though. They sedated her so that I could get some meditation in."

"Did you?"

"Yeah, about six hours worth. My face is all sunburnt and itchy."

"Are you all right?"

"Yeah, I pushed fluids and the gnomes brought me AfterBurn. I'll be fine once I moult."

He kissed her gently on the nose. "Your astral form isn't burned."

"No, and it didn't actually have sex either. Wait. Did I just send a power wave out when I came?"

"You did indeed."

"And you knew I would?" *His expression was answer enough. She stood and deliberately, but lightly put her foot on his cock for balance.* "Thanks *for letting me make an even bigger target of myself."* Sullen and disappointed, she returned to the guestroom.

So they wanted to provoke a response from her stalker. She had just the idea.

Chapter Twenty-Five

"Seesee, you are about to be subjected to my new resolution to get this over with." Abby strode into the gorgon's home with none of the apology that she had shown to Laura.

"Thank god. I do better with a plan of attack. What do you need me to do?" Her hair was wild, happy and hyper at the same time. She looked good, cheerful and relaxed with her *self* free at home.

A blush flared in Abby's face. "I need to be pointed to a room where I can have privacy and be left alone for a few hours."

"Right this way. Do you need anything?"

"Nope. But after this, I am going to make a run for the shower. Ignore any noises you hear, please." Steeling herself for the ordeal to come, she moved into the comfortable and well-appointed room. With a wave to her friend, she closed the door. Her bags and backpack hit the floor and, after a flying leap, she writhed on the bed. "I don't know if I can do this."

The sheets tangled and her arm hit the headboard, the flare of pain made her hiss, but she also felt the surge of power. Aww, hell...

Lust brought on her power, but she couldn't masturbate. The scabs on her hands rubbed against the skin of her belly as she tried to get herself *in the mood*, but it still wasn't working. It was like foreplay with an alligator. She tugged her shirt back down and contemplated her next move. It would have to be something to key her adrenaline. Not just lust. Xander seemed to be the trigger for that.

She crept to the door, opened it and yelled, "Boo!" Interesting. A gnome could go straight into the air for about two feet. "Sorry, Harby.

It was an experiment." She leaned down to give him a short cuddle. This time he didn't unhook her bra, but he was still glaring at her as she patted him on the head and proceeded down the hall.

"What was that about?" Seesee was watching her exiting the guest room with no little amount of surprise.

"I tried an idea that I had, but it didn't work out." Abby exposed her palms to the gorgon. "I didn't put these into the plan." She let a little bit of a whine enter her voice, "Since I have been thwarted, can I get some breakfast?"

Seesee laughed. "Of course. Your creatures have taken over the kitchen already."

She had to wince. "Don't eat anything that I haven't tasted first. The gnomes have a funny sense of humour. They think I will be safest if you are unconscious."

Astonishment was evident until the rueful laughter took its place. "They are probably correct. Until your powers are stable, you are in danger from the vast majority of magical creatures."

"So Xander is fond of telling me." It was a little disturbing that Seesee had not denied being a danger to her. She followed her host into the kitchen and sure enough, there were the gnomes, preparing a feast.

Idly, Abby wondered if they ever ate. She had never seen them eat, but they really knew their way around a kitchen. Orange juice was being squeezed and eggs whipped. Their tiny hands worked with efficiency, each gnome taking on one task, one portion of the assembly line to create the breakfast for their creator and her host.

Mitsy tried to serve Seesee first and, with a heavy sigh, Abby reached out to take a forkful of omelette, only to have her hand smacked to keep the food from her mouth. "Guys, I told you to stop drugging my hosts. If they are going to do me in, it is going to happen regardless of what you do."

Mitsy hung her head in shame, and in a subdued manner, the rest of them plated up the remaining food, to leave it on one large plate with smaller empty ones to the side. The implication that Abby got was that they were to eat from one plate to prove the innocence of the sustenance before them. Tricky little buggers.

"You weren't kidding, were you?"

"Nope. Juice?" She had the glass in her hand and a chagrined Harby claimed it from her and dumped it into the sink. "Do you think water would be safe?" Splint hobbled over to the refrigerator and climbed up to the water carafe, Skint stood beneath with a bucket and they emptied it out while Abby buried her head in her hands.

"They are quick, aren't they?" Seesee was appalled, but had a grudging respect for their efforts to safeguard Abby. It was apparent by her expression.

"Yes. Yes, they are." When the food was finally sorted and Abby confirmed that it was un-tampered with, they had a belated and somewhat cool breakfast.

"Their cooking is excellent." Seesee wiped her mouth on a napkin. "How did you come to animate them?"

With Seesee's earlier comment on not being able to trust her echoing in her mind, she told her what she felt was safe. Not that Xander had shown up and her hormones had triggered a magical wave. That was not something she needed to put on her business card. "Uh, Xander and I have not figured out that one. Fear and tension do seem to have an effect."

"So you were going to cause yourself pain earlier?"

Did the *little death* count as pain? "Yes. That was my plan. I wanted to send out a few large waves of power to make the stalker make their next move immediately. I don't have much patience for this type of thing."

"Ah, do you have another plan?"

"Sort of. How many scary movies do you have on hand? I mean fear inducing ones, not just splatter fests."

"Hmm...a few." Her hair was writhing with excitement.

"Is that because I want to let off a pulse with you right next to me?" Abby gestured to the wild dance that Seesee's hair was doing.

"Yep."

She followed her host into the living room and took the preferred seat for watching the big screen television. She would be truly immersed in the films. She hoped that it was a solid plan. Abby hated horror movies.

Chapter Twenty-Six

"I AM NEVER DOING THAT AGAIN." ABBY'S STOMACH WAS STILL roiling in panic, her nerves vibrated and her host shook under the sheer volume of energy that she had emitted. "I think I am going to be sick."

"Put your head between your knees and breathe." Seesee was amused.

Abby fought the urge to punch her. "If I catch that little bugger, he is going to regret the day he came to life."

Throughout the movies, Harbinger had taken it into his head to touch her with a clammy, wet glove from behind her, under her or on her side. No body part had been safe from his creepy assault. His attacks had been carefully orchestrated. He waited until she was completely immersed in the tension of the films before he touched her, and his light and unpleasant touch had the desired effect. Power had swirled and eventually she had enough for a magical burst. And another and another.

By the end of the third movie, she had let out four waves of energy involuntarily and was exhausted. "Can I take a little nap here? I think I need to recharge a bit."

"Sure, no problem. My hair hasn't felt this lively in ages." The hair in question was tucking a polar fleece blanket around Abby on the chair. It lightly stroked her forehead and left her to sleep.

She must have napped for about an hour, woken only by the shout in the room right in front of her.

"Let me go, you little twits!" Imagine if you will a woman with graceful locks that reached to her waist. Then imagine five garden gnomes fighting that hair in an effort to keep the gorgon from using the camera in her hands.

"It's okay guys, let her go." Shaking off the fatigue that still rode her, she sat up. Rubbing her face to wake herself, he just had to ask, "What were you doing with the camera?"

"I didn't think you would mind and some of my relatives work for the Eternal Archive." At Abby's confused look, she filled in the blank. "There is a reward for the first picture of a Nexus. In the old days it included painting."

"Why would you want to claim the reward?" A bit of hurt crept into her tone, she couldn't help it.

Seesee looked offended. "Of course I wouldn't want to collect the reward, but if I had this picture, no one else could ever submit the *first* picture of you. There are safeguards to protect against fakes in the Archive."

"So what you are saying is that if you take the first picture of me, then no one else will bother seeking one for this archive of yours?" When the gorgon nodded, Abby mulled it over for a minute. "All right, I want a picture with all of my gnomes. We started this together after all. Gather around guys."

She fought herself free of the blanket and knelt on the carpet, gesturing for her gnomes to surround her. When they remained at Seesee's feet, she did a head count. "Where is Bitsy?"

"Which one is Bitsy?" Looking around, she obviously didn't see anything amiss.

"He's the dwarf gnome. I was running out of wire to make his skeleton and so he ended up half the height of the others." The other gnomes looked worried.

"I haven't seen him. Do they know where he has gotten to?"

"Harby? Mitsy? Ruffles? Skint? Splint? Have you seen him? Do you know where he is?" Her position on the floor made asking them easy, but at the same time, she was hoping that he was just playing the kind of joke that Harby had been during the movie. Her blood pounded in her veins and her body flexed as each gnome shook their heads to indicate a lack of knowledge of the whereabouts of their little brother.

Abby rose to her feet and concentrated. If she could just focus on her power, the power that the gnomes carried and find its match, she may be able to find her precious little one.

"What are you doing, Abby?" Seesee was behind her and sounded like she was a thousand worlds away.

"I am tracking Bitsy with the traces of my power still within him." She looked from one end of the house to the other, looking through walls and seeking power.

"You can do that?"

"We will see." There. A glimmer, a flicker. Faint but tantalizing. "I found him. Stay here."

"What? No!"

Her gnomes were keeping Seesee occupied, the scrambling behind her was comforting. She would be alone. Seesee's access to the backyard was done through a regular door of wood and glass, the small spells woven into the doorjamb were no deterrent to her exit.

The yard was well tended and Seesee did love her roses. It was under a blood rose bush that Abby found her tiny companion. "Oh, Bitsy. What happened to you?" His energy signature had been faint because there was a giant hole in it. Someone or something had plucked out one third of his life force. Bastards.

He was firmly curled around the base of the rose bush. His bright blue eyes met hers through the thorny brambles that guarded him. He was in pain. Incredible pain. "I know you are hurting, sweetie. I can help you, but you have to trust me. Come out, Bitsy, I promise you will be safe today." She only hoped she wasn't lying.

Slowly, with motions that spoke of his agony, he crawled out toward her. She waited until his body was completely exposed before she gently lifted him to cradle him against her chest. Power flowed into the void within him, she poured all her energy into him until he breathed more easily. As she cradled him, she rocked back and forth, humming to him. She had moved through her entire repertoire of 80's pop songs and was revisiting *Girls Just Wanna Have Fun* when he fought her grip and sat up.

Teary, they looked at each other and he tugged on his vest. She didn't know how she had missed it, but there was a folded piece of paper safety pinned to his vest.

This was not going to be good. She had a funny feeling.

Chapter Twenty-Seven

BITSY WAS ON PATROL AND HE SAW SOMETHING HE DIDN'T LIKE. With the rest of his family watching the Nexus, he was concentrating on the unusual goings on down the street. The human was knocking on the door of the magus. He welcomed her with an uncomfortable smile, but took the coffee cup that she brought him. She followed him into the house, but left the door open. This wasn't good.

Bitsy scurried closer to the still-open door. Inside the two were standing and talking when suddenly the magus began to sway. He couldn't hear them, but it didn't matter, the human caught him under the arm and walked him out of the door. He was on the ground on his back by the time she got him to the sidewalk.

He watched in astonishment as the smallish human dragged the magus by his heels toward the Nexus' home. Up the stairs and through the house she went. She used the keys that she had had before the Nexus moved in and dragged the magus through the house.

Curious beyond belief, Bitsy followed. If he could help the magus in any way, he would. But with Xander being unconscious, there wasn't much that he could actually do. He could only lift twenty pounds.

Keeping to the shadows, he entered his home. It didn't greet him like it had taken to doing. Something was killing it, draining it of life and magic. If he wasn't careful, the same could happen to him. Caution now ran through him as he moved. The human was doing something that she shouldn't be able to. It couldn't be the magus, he was out cold.

The sunlight in the backyard was off its peak. Noon had come and gone. Crushed grass showed the way to the tree where the magus was being fastened. The great oak didn't like being used as a method of confinement and sent its complaint out across the magical ether. Bitsy thought to himself that he may be able to fix that. Whatever was holding the magus up, could be undone, if only he could get himself close enough.

It was with that goal in mind that he inched around the yard, hiding in the shadows and under the new bushes that they had spent all that time planting to disguise their tunnel entrance.

He wasn't expecting to be caught with his hands on the cuffs tying the magus to the tree and he certainly wasn't expecting the other human to touch him in the chest, bringing pain the likes of which no gnome should have felt.

Agony seared him. The magic that gave him his life was bleeding away and there was nothing that he could do about it. The human pinned something to him.

"Give that you your mistress before you die, magical filth."

Sent on his way, it took all of his energy to crawl the length of the Nexus' yard, through the mermaid's property and to make it to the gorgon's home. He slumped exhausted under the rose bushes and hoped for the best. The Nexus would find him, but he hoped it would be in time to save the life he was coming to love.

Chapter Twenty-Eight

"**D**ID YOU FIND HIM?" SEESEE WAS STILL BLOCKED FROM THE DOOR by the gnomes, but the concern in her voice wasn't faked. Mitsy was dangling in her tresses and didn't look too pleased about it.

"I did. Someone chewed a hole in him."

The gnomes instantly abandoned Seesee to cluster around Abby and Bitsy as they made their way to the kitchen table. "I patched him up with most of the magic that I had, but he is still bleeding energy."

"Who do you think did it?"

Bitsy was being treated to hugs and cuddles as he was coddled by his family. He met Abby's gaze with his own and nodded.

She unfolded the paper that she had clenched in her fist. The contents shocked her anew and the handwriting was terribly familiar. "You need to call everyone in the neighbourhood and bring them here. Now."

"Why?"

"Because I know who is doing this and it has to stop." Bitsy was running low so she topped him up. The drain was still occurring and was showing no signs of stopping.

Someone needed their ass kicked.

SEESEE HAD CALLED ALL the neighbours together after she had read the note. The sun had set and darkness enveloped the cul-de-sac that they called home. It guarded their movements and those of anyone who would harm the new Nexus.

Only two people were absent and those absences said enough.

She faced the inhabitants of Oak Point Way and spoke her peace. "Ladies and gentleman. I have called you here to announce that the stalker has taken a hostage."

An excited murmur broke through their shock.

"One of my gnomes was taken and drained of magic and a note was pinned to his vest. He was left to die and would have if we hadn't realized that he was missing."

A concerned note ran through the group. "What was on the note?"

"It's a message. For me." She nodded at her audience. "There is something that I have to do and if I don't return in two hours, leave Oak Point Way. You will have no reason to be here any longer."

"Are you going to kill yourself?" Verne was shocked. That would be the only reason that they would leave. If she was dead. It was chilling to have it out that clearly.

"Oh God, no! But I may get my ass kicked, be burned out, or what-have-you. If I do, this someone may die, and if I don't do this, people are guaranteed to die."

Laura frowned. "This is a little cryptic, Abby."

"I know, but I have to say goodnight to the gnomes and then be on my way."

"You do realize that we have to stop you." That one was Verne.

"And I do realize that you all have had some of the iced tea that the gnomes brought you when you arrived. You should be limp for about an hour." She stood and made her way to the front door. "I am sorry and I hope to see you all soon." They were indeed all slumping over. She didn't know if the sedative would last for an hour, but she was glad that they would not be endangered.

And she was scared shitless of what was about to go down.

EXTENSIVE RESEARCH ON THE internet proved what Harby had suspected, the mistress was in control of wild magic. That was why someone was trying to kill her.

It was considered the most dangerous and unstable type of magic because it could adhere to anything. It could stick to a tree, branch, lamppost or car, even a house. Nothing could stop it. It would do what it willed with no rules or regulations, and that is what it was doing now.

Fortunately for the gnomes, one of the inhabitants of Oak Point Way had an open internet network, with no passwords, which allowed them to jump the signal with no one the wiser. If they had been human, they may have had a twinge of guilt, but as it was, Harby spent long hours online researching BDSM. Wondering to himself why the mistress had crafted him in such a way. And then he remembered, she thought it was funny.

He had already enacted some of the urges that dwelled within him with Mitsy and Ruffles but when he tried it with Skint, he was out of luck. The naked gnome was far too slippery.

With the Nexus safely ensconced in the gorgon's home, they took up positions to guard their mistress. Bitsy was on point, outdoors, reconnoitring, which is why no one noticed that he had disappeared.

When the Nexus went out to retrieve him and brought him back to them, they felt his pain. The hole in his life force that was draining him dry. It was a testament to the magic of the Nexus that without willing it, she had bound them together in body and soul.

Harby could feel Bitsy's betrayal and bitter disappointment in his own skills. His family could only let him work it out as the power drain continued.

For the first time since they had come alive, they followed the mistress's orders by not following her. She had commanded them to sedate the inhabitants of Oak Point Way, and they had. She demanded that they watch the slumbering neighbours, and they did.

They were only waiting for their chance to assist their mistress, but Bitsy's injury proved a point, they were no match for the evil that was stalking the mistress. Instead, they gave her the only weapon at their disposal.

WITH HER HAND TREMBLING, she moved to open the front door and was once again hampered by a pyramid of gnomes. Bitsy was not part of the pyramid, but instead moved to her and handed her a tiny scrap of paper. She knelt down to examine it.

It was a map of her backyard. The detail was exquisite, right down to the stick figure tied to the tree and a large red X next to the oak in one of the flowerbeds. She pointed to it. "What is mark in the flowers?"

With a solemn look at her, Bitsy simply said, "Boom."

For the first time since she had seen him under the roses, Abby smiled. There just might be some hope out there after all. "Stay here and help the others when they come out of it, all right?" At the tiny ring of nods, she smiled and went out to be the Nexus.

Chapter Twenty-Nine

Abby fought the urge to whistle. It would have broken the tension that she was experiencing. Or it would have pissed off the squirrel in the tree above her, either one would have been good.

The street was silent. No one was out, they were all slumped over at Seesee's house. The frisson of guilt washed over her and she let it go. It wouldn't serve her in any way to beat her chest and it might get Xander killed.

Her house was dark, silent, creepy, and she needed to mow the lawn. Perhaps if they survived this, she could convince Xander to do it for her, shirtless of course. That little lustful thought sent a curl of magic through her, but she needed more if Bitsy's injury was an example of the kind of damage that could be done. She stood for a moment as she moved into the once-familiar home that she loved. Something was different.

"Xander? Are you in here?" Abby crept into the dark stillness of her own home and waited. There was no reply, no sound at all. It was eerie. For the last few weeks, she had had the incessant noise of the gnomes running through her house. She missed their psychotic cheer.

The glow-in-the-dark figurines that she had unpacked upon moving in lit her way. She used the figures to orient herself in the complete darkness. Even her coffeemaker lights were out. Something had cut the power. It looked like her stalker was escalating.

The note that she had been given had been very specific.

I have your boyfriend. If you want him to live, you will come to the oak in your backyard and meet me without any of your creatures. After sundown. If I see one stubby hand, Alexander Desmith dies.

P.S. Make sure that none of your power leaks or you will find him missing one limb for each time you lose control. Come alone.

There was no signature, but the spidery script was crystal clear. Abby shivered to realize that Xander's kidnapper had dragged him through her hallways only hours before. She still didn't know how Xander had been taken, but his abductor obviously had overpowered him.

The energy in her home was gone. Completely drained. Could the abductor have done the same to Xander? Wait. The power wasn't drained, it was drain*ing*. She used her newly trained senses to follow the energy without expending any of her own. It was flowing in a column to the oak in her backyard. Well, hell. The gnomes had it right.

"SO YOU DRUGGED MY coffee?" He struggled against the cuffs binding him to the tree. They were not moving.

"It was so easy. You never suspected a thing." His abductor swung one foot idly in the air from her perch on the bench.

"How did you dampen my powers? I have never felt anything like that." He was trying to distract her, Abby would come, he was sure and this predator was lying in wait. It was driving him nuts. The rough bark of the oak was rubbing his spine raw. He had spent the last few minutes surreptitiously trying to work one of his hands out of the handcuff. It was no use. They were on far too tightly to enable that manoeuvre.

"I was born to absorb the power that you arrogantly call magic. It runs into me like a river whenever I am around it and I will drain Abby dry. I have never been able to drain a Nexus before. I think I will enjoy this." She rubbed her hands together in anticipation. "But first, I am going to make sure that you don't distract me in my purpose." A few sharp jerks and his mouth was duct taped.

Well, hell. She was nuts.

THE SLOPE LEADING DOWN to the oak tree was lit by tiki torches, a nice touch. Miranda must have brought her own. Just to give it a spooky feel. Creepy. Creepy and tacky.

As the gnomes had indicated Xander was tied to the tree, but from this distance, she could only see that he was shirtless. Damn. How did that psycho get his shirt off?

Sliding open and deliberately closing the glass patio door bought her a little time to calm herself. This was going to be sink or swim. Laura would appreciate that one.

"Ah, the great and powerful Nexus! How kind of you to join us." Miranda Simmons was cheerful. She had some weird dagger with her and was looking distinctly pleased with herself.

Abby kept walking toward the nut with her back to the river.

"Are you prepared to die?"

"That depends, are you prepared to let Xander go?"

A cackle cracked through the air. "No. He stays until your power is tapped out and your heart has stopped beating." She waggled the dagger in the air.

"Uh, if you are going to kill me, why don't you get it over with and shoot me?"

Miranda looked a little impatient. "Based on my lack of success in hitting you with a car or blowing you up, I feel that the best way to kill you is up close and personal. Without any mechanical intervention."

"Okay, I have to admit that you have a valid point." She crossed her arms, but still stayed about fifteen feet away from the knife wielding nut-o-naut. "Did you know that I could deflect that stuff? Because I surely didn't. A fucking *car* for god's sake."

"I tried to get to you before your powers fell under your control." She paced restlessly.

Abby moved closer to Xander.

"How was I to know that Xander was going to tutor you so extensively?"

"He did show me several things that I hadn't seen before. Especially during the tutoring sessions at my home." Xander's weary face lit with a smile behind the tape and he shook against his chains. The distraction was enough for Abby to have her toe connect with the oak root that was under her foot.

Miranda brandished her knife at Xander. "Keep quiet, Xander. You will have your turn."

Phase one was now complete. Phase two was a little more difficult. "Are you going to kill the other inhabitants of the neighbourhood as well? Including Xander?"

"No, of course not. I simply need to kill you so that the plague that you spread will be stopped. Xander needs to be punished a bit before I let him go though. If he hadn't been so obsessed with you, you would be dead already." Her confidence that she would not be punished was proof of her madness. She honestly seemed to think that everything would go back the way it was.

Abby fixated on the one word that caught her attention. "Plague?"

"Magic. Or what passes for magic nowadays."

There was a lot of loathing in those words. "I thought you were from a magical family? Why do you hate it?"

"I have always been a second class citizen. My own family is embarrassed by my existence. I have never felt like I belonged." The shudder that ran through her was more true emotion than she had ever shown before. And here it was all due to family feuding. What a surprise.

"I understand." She really did. It echoed her own experience with her family.

"How could you? You have all the power in two worlds at your disposal!"

She did? Cool, she would have to put that on her business card. "I have been shunned by my mother's family. I was always too low class for them. Never the right job or the right address. Saved me a lot of money on Christmas presents, I can tell you."

"So that is why you are willing to walk into my knife?"

"No. That is why I don't want anyone else to be hurt. The people here are good, no matter their magical status. They have been friends and helped me when there was no reason to. That alone is my reason for being here." The truth in her words surprised even herself. "That brings me to another point. Can you drain the Nexus energy without touching that of the others?"

"Of course I can."

A deep breath and a longing look at Xander, with as much warning as she could put into her eyes, and she nodded. "Then let's rock."

Chapter Thirty

THE PROCESS WAS NOT PAINLESS. NOT BY A LONG SHOT. BITSY must have been in agony.

It took all the energy that she had just to keep from shrieking in panic and running for the safety of her house. A deep breath and a mental recitation of her plan let her stay fixed to the ground.

As it was the first sharp tug on her magic actually made her stumble forward a few steps. She tried to retreat, but the energy that bound her to Miranda was stretchy, like taffy and kept snapping back.

"You have so much more power than I had imagined. No wonder I couldn't kill you by surprise." She sounded like she had stumbled across a cheesecake buffet.

"Are you simply drawing my magic? The taste of the Nexus magic is what you are aiming for, right?"

Miranda was pacing again.

Abby tried to keep her from detecting the location of the power that she was drawing. Idle chitchat in the face of agony and torture should work.

"Of course, I am. I have control over my talent. Too bad you could not say the same." And with that Miranda flung her arms wide and let the power of the Nexus flow into her.

With her inner eye, Abby could see her power moving toward the black hole that was Miranda. It disappeared into her, but she could still feel it, moving and fighting the darkness.

The flowerbed heaved. The thick bubble of magic was dissolving rapidly, and Miranda was standing right in front of it. This was going to be good.

It only took twenty-three seconds for her to *eat* the bubble. And only three seconds for the *boom* to flatten everything in sight.

The draining had already weakened her knees so Abby was able to drop to the ground and lie flat as the blast wave washed over her.

Miranda was not so fortunate. The rampaging psycho was flat on her face, evidence of the garden exploding, all over her back.

As Abby investigated, it seemed that a begonia was now firmly lodged in Miranda's butt. The jokes were too terrible.

Her magic had returned to her in a rush, but no amount of magic on her part would get Xander off that tree. The oak had shielded him from the blast, using its roots and branches to take the brunt of the debris.

"Hey, Xander. I just have to find the keys for those cuffs." She frisked Miranda's unconscious body and it was in the third pocket that she found them. "I'll have you out of there in a minute. I got the keys."

While Abby worked at the cuffs in the limited lighting, she heard a tiny stampede and looked over to find the gnomes carrying Miranda up the hill, the begonia waving proudly from her ass. A flag on the battleground.

She opened the left cuff first, arm, then leg and the leg and then the wrist of the right side. Just so he wouldn't fall down as so often depicted in the movies and cartoons.

With a grimace and a wince, Xander tore the tape from his mouth. "Abby, if you ever do anything that stupid again, I am going to paddle you for a week."

Abby looked at him for a long time. "If I am ever in the position to do something like this, I'll let them kill you first, then take my turn. Is that okay?"

He glared at her. Bruised and insulted, he took the only course of action open to him. He kissed her.

Abby wrapped her hands around his neck and pulled him into her with everything in her. "This was the reason that I risked my life, just this. My life has been turned on its head, everything I thought wasn't real, is and then there is you. You are the same man that I met the first day. The same man that   made my heart pound and gave me the energy to bring the gnomes to life just by walking through my house." Her lips duelled with his again, then pulled away. "For that I will risk anything."

He looked down at her as he kept her close enough for her to feel his appreciation of her speech. "For that I am humbled, and grateful, and still really, really pissed off."

"Oh, dear, is there anything that I can do to take out the sting of it?"

His hands wrapped around her waist and he rocked his hips against her. "I think you may just have to work it off."

"Is it a worthy cause?"

"I think so. What do you think it's worth?"

She shifted her hips from side to side against him. "A lot. Quite a bit. I have a large bit of interest in your large bit of interest." A sudden thought occurred to her. "Do you need any extra energy? Did Miranda drain you?"

"Uh, no. She drugged me with coffee."

"But why did you let her in? Your own rules said that no one was to go visiting on the street."

"Uh, Miranda and I used to date. Years ago, just after the street was activated."

Nothing to kill a mood like knowing that it was his ex that had put him and them in danger. "Dare I ask as to why she had the handcuffs?" The flush that was visible on his cheeks was answer enough. "She bound you with stuff from your toy chest. That is twisted." A new side of Xander that she wasn't pleased with. She would have to deal with it another day.

He was gently rubbing at the marks left by the cuffs. "She is a twisted lady. Speaking of which, where is she?"

Okay, it was back to business. "The gnomes took her back to Seesee's. We should probably join them."

"How do you know where the gnomes took her?"

"I can follow that pitter patter of tiny feet. That, and it is where I told them to take her when I was making my plans." She took his arm to support him across the yard. "Don't worry, the others should be waking up shortly."

Xander stopped and looked at her. "What did you do?" His arm snaked around her waist and he gripped her tightly, his worry for his friends obvious. "Are they all okay? Did Miranda do anything?"

"Nope. I took a little help from my friends." She got him moving again, and together they made their way through the darkness and to the only lit home on Oak Point Way. "The gnomes have a way with sedatives. Now let's go wake them up so that Verne can try to kill me again. He really is a one trick pony. Werewolf. Whatever."

Chapter Thirty-One

Seesee's living room was almost as Abby had left it. Almost. The addition of a bound and gagged Miranda was new as was the prone form of Verne on the eastern carpeting. His eyes were open and blinking and, as Abby and Xander entered the room, his gaze became furious.

The gnomes were even giving him a wide berth and that was not a good sign. They weren't afraid of anyone, but Verne had done something to scare them.

"I am sorry that I told them to dope you, but if they used what I think they did, this should burn it off." Abby went from neighbour to neighbour and gave them a shot of the panic-magic that she had generated while Miranda was draining her. When they stirred within two minutes, she had another answer for her growing list of questions. Her power did indeed carry *flavours* with it. And panic magic was a short burn.

"What happened and why did you do that to us?" Seesee was the first one to be revived.

Abby had just finished Laura and was reaching for Verne. Two fingers touched his shoulder and she let the power run between them. "I needed to meet her alone or she said she would hurt Xander and you all." She should have been paying more attention because seconds later, there was a rush of fur under her hand and she again had a snarling wolf at her throat. Xander was in no shape to help her so Seesee's hair whipped out to pull the were from her torso.

"Back off, Verne. I wasn't harmed. Neither were you, so stop being so dramatic."

He slumped in the air where the gorgon was holding him and began to shift back to human before he was back on the ground. "I am sorry, Abby, Miranda's scent tells the truth about her being the stalker, well, that and the marks on Xander's wrists." He was fully back to human now, but still looked a little dizzy.

"Did you put all your energy into the change?" Another point for her list of questions. Now to see if he would give in and let her help.

"Yes. It does take a lot of magic to shift."

"Will you accept more power to take up the loss?"

He shook his head and his stocky body shivered. "Here? Now? The magic you just gave me was enough to power the first shift, but it seems to have worn off."

"Different magic for a different purpose. That was to wake you." She moved toward him again and Seesee had her hair at the ready. "This is to charge you." Abby looked over at Xander and let the warmth of his presence wash through her. It was enough. Verne took her hand and the power moved from her to him. It was a smooth transfer and not the first jolt that had hit Laura. He looked surprised, but smiled as the energy absorbed into his body and light came to his eyes.

"They were right to send us here. Even Miranda had her part to play. I sincerely hoped that they had not known of her plan before she was sent here, and if they did, they must be made to pay." Verne the avenging werewolf was a mercurial change from the beast at her throat a minute ago.

Xander had taken up a seat on the couch and Abby joined him.

"Is she all right?"

His concern cooled her attraction, but then she realized that Miranda hadn't moved yet.

"Yup. She is awake already, although she is really sore."

"How can you tell?"

"I am reading her lack of magic. It is shifting and pulsing, but missing in a few spots. Plus she has started to twitch."

The room at large turned its attention to the figure on the floor and watched her as you would watch an alligator that had entered your house.

"Can you block her talents?" Laura was asking, Verne had taken her into his arms and they were eyeing Miranda with disgust.

"No. If you know anyone who has tranquilizers, that may be best. She can still suck all my power out of me as soon as she can calm down enough, but I don't have any more exploding flowerbeds nearby."

The gnomes were near Miranda's head and poking a hole in the tape they had used with a small knife. They fed a straw to her and she slowly and solemnly drank from the lemonade that they had brought her. She seemed grateful for the attention. The room grew quiet as her breathing slowed and she fell into the soothing darkness of sleep.

"Ordinarily, I wouldn't let them sedate someone, but I feel that Randy is a special case here. At least until someone can find something to do with her." As she spoke, Xander flushed.

"Seesee? May I borrow your phone?" With a groan, he stood and moved into the kitchen at her nod. He was in pain.

Abby had no idea how long he had been shackled to the tree, but it had been more than five minutes and less than six hours. He was stiff, he was sore, but he was safe. Abby counted his blessings for him. The idle thought that with elves in his family, he may have a sensitivity to metal flitted through her mind. Well, he would mention it if he needed extra attention.

The group that was normally so boisterous was ominously silent.

Abby threw in a conversational hot button. "So I know that Miranda here was used to purchase and search out the location where I would want to live, but how did you all decide to come in and join this merry neighbourhood?"

Not one of them was going to answer.

She asked, "Seesee? Why did you end up on the Nexus Neighbourhood Watch?"

Seesee glanced around her for a moment as if looking for an escape. No such luck. "My people *wanted* to send a representative to the seers to see if we had someone suitable."

"Who are your people? Forgive me for my ignorance, but in the histories, there are never more than three gorgons at a time." She had googled the history of gorgons as best she could. The history of mermaids as well.

"That is true. I have two sisters and Melly already has her three daughters. There will be no more this generation. That is what made me a candidate for the Mythology seat on the council to send as a companion for you."

"Wow, so singular creatures are part of your group? Can you name a few?"

Seesee did look pleased at her interest. "There is a Phoenix, a Dragon, a Minotaur—he is our current ambassador to the council—and a Gryphon just joined. There are also some half breeds making a bid for a separate seat, but until they get it, they are lumped in with us."

"That is excellent. Everyone needs to feel that they belong somewhere. It was part of Miranda's problem." They all looked at her. "She felt like a second class magical citizen and she claims to have been treated in just such a manner her whole life. It sucks when that happens." She blotted at her eyes, the thought of being alone in a room full of people who are supposed to love you touched a little close to home. "All right. Seesee was chosen by a seer. How about you, Laura?"

"I was ordered to be here, by my grandmother."

"Right. Is she still alive?"

"She is. And she was insistent that her family be represented here. It was a matter of honour. I did it out of family obligation and have not regretted a moment of it since the day we met. Aside from you sedating us while you wandered off to take on Miranda. That sucked. Don't ever do that again."

Abby grinned. "I think I can guarantee it. I hope I can anyway. If there is another one out there like her, I may just live my life in a bunker." She turned to the wolf man who had twice laid a fang on her. "Verne. Let me guess. You were ordered here by your pack leader."

"You are incorrect. I entered a competition to earn my place in your guard."

Giggles broke out. "You are in my guard and you have attacked me twice? Did you read the job description at all?" His chagrined face was too precious. The giggles turned into peals of laughter.

"I am sorry I failed you. At your word, you can have my replacement here."

"Am I correct in assuming that the attacks were spurred by your over abundance of Nexus magic? Nod your head to say yes." She was nodding her head in exaggeration and he finally got the hint.

"Yes. I went wolf and was slightly out of control."

"Well, because I was also out of control, no harm done. In fact, your instinct to guard the other victim of the power burst was appropriate and heroic." There. They had officially dealt with his attacking her to defend Laura and they hadn't even needed The People's Court to do it.

Whew.

Xander came back into the room and nodded to let Seesee know that someone wanted to speak with her.

She picked up the phone with puzzlement and then jumped to her feet. "Hello Councilman. Yes, Councilman. Completely powerless, Councilman. She can drain anything else, sir. The Nexus is fine, sir. As are her creatures, sir. I look forward to it as well, sir." She hung up the phone and dropped onto the couch, causing Abby to bounce slightly. A bemused Seesee sat and looked up at Xander. "The powerless transporters are being *sent* to your house. They will be here in a few minutes."

Xander looked a little shocked, as if two strangers were just going to materialize in his home. Abby was surprised by his concern, "Hey, they aren't just going to pop into your home, are they?"

"If the council is sending them, they certainly are." Verne nodded wisely. "It is the fastest way. We are all magical and useless for long transport of one such as Miranda. Besides, I will need to be there to work them through customs."

Xander nodded. "And I will have to be there to air the events at the council. To make sure that Miranda is properly kept in custody without magic to drain. I am just concerned because I left a few of the cursed objects out. I don't want them setting them off."

He was going to leave. The danger was over and he was leaving her. She tried not to be hurt, tried to keep her feelings to herself and ended up just walking out of the room and collecting her backpack and sleeping bag.

It was time to go home.

Chapter Thirty-Two

She was halfway to her sanctum when Xander caught up with her. The flare of magic in his home had him cursing and he looked at her with an urgency that she couldn't read. He grabbed her and gave her a kiss to curl her toes, then murmured, "I will be back," and ran to his house before the unmagical ones started picking up cursed objects.

"Great. When will that be? After I have been eaten by a gargoyle?" She was not muttering to herself, her *creatures* had taken up an honour guard around her. Bitsy was leading the way, and a close look with her inner eye, let her know that his leak was no more. Apparently, Miranda's draining link had been broken when she had been blasted by the begonia. "Well, I know at least one thing that you guys will be doing. I am guessing that I have a rather large hole in the backyard right now. You wouldn't want to take care of that, would you?" Excited squeals greeted her speech. They were definitely more verbal.

The door to her house opened as they approached, it hadn't been completely drained either. Lights came on and she breathed deeply, running her surplus magic into her home, feeling it greet her in response. She was home.

She was surrounded by her creatures, backed by a home that welcomed her and a message blinking on her answering machine. What the hell?

"Abby, it's Tina. Your Gnomes are doing great things out there. People love the poses and the scenes. What I want to know is, when can I get your next book? What have you been working on out there in

Sargent? Call me." The beep took her by surprise.

A new book? Another group of creatures? Her herd had moved into the house and she heard the back door slide open and shut. Groundskeeping at midnight? What the heck, it wasn't like they needed the sleep.

She needed sleep. Her body was tired, there was dirt in her hair and nails. The scabs on her hands had torn open and she could feel the itch of blood as she moved through her house. Blood never killed anything. Well, unless she lost all of it and that would not happen tonight.

She moved into the bathroom, and at seeing her face, decided that a shower was in order before bed. Her sheets would never forgive her otherwise.

The water came up to heat slowly, and it was only when she was standing under the blast that she realized that she was crying. It had taken almost getting killed, almost having her gnomes in danger and almost losing Xander to make her realize that this was really her life. The only life that she would live.

It was not a dream.

Nothing about this was a dream.

Her friends were a mermaid and a creature of myth and the mermaid's suitor was a werewolf who answered to the magus next door.

No wonder Miranda hadn't fit in, no sane human could. So where did that leave Abby?

Chapter Thirty-Three

"ALL RIGHT YOU TWO. I WANT YOUR STORIES, AND I WANT THEM from the beginning. Laura, you first. How the heck did you get sent here? This is a land-locked province for the most part."

Her two friends looked at each other and shrugged. With Xander taking off unceremoniously the night before, they had come over the instant that Abby had called, fearing that she was going to have some sort of breakdown. And she did. Sort of.

"Are you sure that you want to know all this now? You don't want to ask about the trial for Miranda?"

"No. I most definitely do not want to talk about Miranda. Nope. Not at all." She crossed her arms over her breasts and glared at the mermaid. "Now, spill. Where were you when you first got the call? Did you get to pick your home? Decorate it? Who lived here before?"

Laura took a deep breath and humoured her. "Um. I guess I was off the coast of Newfoundland when I was summoned by my grandmother."

"Summoned, how? Did she use semaphore? Psychic powers? How?" She knew that they were going to humour her after her shock and she was taking full advantage by asking the questions that she had been afraid would be impolite.

"Uh, yeah. I suppose that psychic powers are a good description. She is the matriarch of our clan so she can reach any of us at a moment's notice."

"Handy."

"Not when you are with a guy." The smile that Laura gave her almost thawed her. Almost. She couldn't forget that at this moment

Xander and two guys she hadn't met were across the border and delivering Miranda to members of a magical council for assessment. He hadn't even said goodbye.

Wiener.

Based on the looks she was getting, her bad mood was back on her face. "Okay, so the matriarch has the power to call you. What happened then?"

"I swam to her home and then was told that a new Nexus had been discovered and that the council had decided that a multi-racial honour guard was needed. Our clan had been selected for the mer representation and Grandma had picked me."

"How many relatives did she have to choose from?"

"Two hundred and forty-seven." At Abby's goggle-eyed look, she clarified, "One hundred don't speak English and seventy-five don't like to walk on land."

"So. You were chosen out of seventy-two?"

"Yep. Gran had me selected the instant she found out about our clan's selection. I am the youngest granddaughter that she has. She wants to make me a more attractive mate for some merman. A connection to the Nexus will do that."

"Thank you. That was very honest of you. So how long did it take you to move in?"

"Well, my people used the river system and everything was delivered here in a matter of weeks. Because of my nature, I got the home with the pool and the pearl icons coating the walls are still alive. They are some of the treasures of the deep that I was able to bring with me so I wouldn't get homesick."

"Your family moved you in?" Nostalgia was in her tone. She couldn't help it. She had had to depend on the kindness of strangers. How Southern. She almost smacked herself in the head. "Who was here when you moved in?"

"Uh, the realtor. Miklos was in the house at the end of the street. I was here on my own for about a month before Verne and Seesee showed up."

The realtor was now code for Miranda. It was too bad that the name rubbed her raw, but the woman had tried to kill her. Three times. Four, if you counted the attack on her ex-apartment. Miranda hadn't copped to it, but it had to have been her out to smash the gnomes before anything could happen.

"When will I meet Miklos? He seems to be gone an awful lot."

Seesee flushed a heady bronze. "He will be here by the next full moon. With Verne incapacitated at the moon and Xander at the council, he is the protector to the gateway."

"Gateway? You mean Oak Point Way?"

"Something like that. The street is actually enchanted against unmagical interference."

"Then how does the mail arrive?"

"The mailman is a half-demon who requested assignment to this area to make you more secure."

"What about the river flowing behind my home? Someone could come in there?" This was more interesting that she had thought. She had just meant to taunt them to make them spill info. Now they were answering questions with topics she wanted to know about.

"The stones out back have been warded to prevent unwanted visitors. They were enchanted by a consortium of witches who were chosen at random with only power being the main concern. It is wrapped up tighter than a toddler's diaper."

"Eww. And on that note, Seesee, tell me about yourself. How did you get chosen from all of the mythical creatures that were available?"

Seesee stalled for a moment by getting herself a cup of coffee that she had made for herself, declining the offer of Mitsy to make coffee for their little group.

So she got smarter. Good for her. "Spill it, Montrose. How did you end up being the *chosen one*?"

Her skin was darkening rapidly. "I slept with the minotaur to get the assignment."

Laura led the shrieking. "What!"

Abby was close behind with, "Holy Hell!" She recovered quickly.

"Was he hung like a bull?" Her eyebrows were moving manically, but she couldn't stop them."

"Well, the mythical creature's seat on the council is more of a courtesy than a voting seat so we are a lot less formal. Vokal was voted in to represent us for the next three years, but if I am linked to the Nexus guard, I can run for the representative spot."

"So in an effort to gain political leverage, you banged a bull?"

Her hands were now over her face, but they could understand the mumble, "Something like that."

"How was it?" Laura was being practical, good for her.

Another sigh from the hands. "He was very inventive. I was on top so he wouldn't crush me and he really liked my hair being prehensile. Is that enough?"

An evil cackle broke free of Abby's throat, surprising even her. "We will wait until you're drunk before we ask if he was circumcised."

"Oh, goddess." Seesee suddenly met Abby's gaze. "Did your gnomes put any truth serum in the food?"

"Nope. There is no food and you made the coffee. I guess you wanted to get that off your chest."

"I guess I did. Well, I got the vote to come here as the mythical creature representative, I selected the home that seemed most comfortable to me. Number Thirteen had been reserved for you and so I selected the house between Miranda and Laura's. My sisters and my nieces came to help me move in. So did Vokal, which was kind and creepy at the same time."

"Does he think it was more than a one night stand?"

"Uh, we weren't standing."

"Ha ha. You know what I mean."

"He has a harem of his own so I don't think so. He just wanted to see where the next Nexus was going to live."

That made sense, she supposed, but then she had another thought. "You both have businesses and Verne works for customs, was that all set up, too?"

From both ladies, "Yes."

Seesee explained, "We needed to integrate into Sargent as quickly as we could so we were given businesses that would increase the local economy and set us up as valuable members of the community. Over the centuries, magical creatures have found that being useful is a way to insure that the non-magical persons accept us in their midst."

"Laura has an aquarium? Right?"

"Yup. It serves as more of an Agony Aunt shop. People come in to tell me how their fish die. It is kind of morbid, but it has bonded me to at least a third of the population. And if I can make the lives of their little fish more comfortable, it's my duty to help."

"That is very altruistic of you. Can you understand fish?"

"Occasionally. If they are in a large enough group. But the individuals keep to themselves."

"I did not know that about fish. Thank you."

"You are welcome."

Silence fell heavily between them for a moment until Seesee reached for a bag that was on the floor next to her. "Okay, time for chocolate." A vast array of goodies began to appear on the counter as Seesee unloaded the box that was inside the bag. And then another and then another.

"Uh, ladies. I am really sorry about sedating you, but can you assure me that I am not going to keel over or turn blue or something? I like to think that it is in the past, at least when the gnomes are out in the yard."

Seesee pondered her words for a looooonnnnggg moment. "Avoid the éclairs."

"But they are my favourite!"

"And they are coated with chocolate Exlax."

"I will avoid the éclairs." She was completely solemn for a moment and then burst out giggling, grabbing for one of the tiny cheesecakes with a blueberry topping. The éclairs were shunned one at a time, being placed on the edge of the counter for later disposal.

It was a shame, but better than the alternative.

After their third cups of coffee and tea respectively, Abby figured that she could continue the questioning. "Laura, this one has been bugging me since I first met you."

"Shoot."

"Why don't you and Verne formalize your relationship? You seem to be holding him at bay for some reason and I can't figure it out."

Seesee was all ears. "I have to admit that I have been curious myself. You two suit each other more than any other couple I have seen, but you seem to keep a barrier between you."

Laura stirred her tea and the twist of her lips indicated her decision making. "Verne and I are complicated."

"I have noticed." Abby couldn't stop the eye roll. It went with the sarcastic tone.

"He is a werewolf and they mate for life." She met the eyes of her two companions. "But I am a mermaid and will live for five hundred years. His lifespan and mine are two very different things."

All right, so it wasn't a difference of religion or anything. "Wow. That is a problem. What about kids?"

"Mer children need to be in water for their first five years before they can shift to a form that will have oxygen breathing lungs."

"What if they were born as were? Would they be able to shift to either form?"

"No one has ever dared to try it. The risk to the offspring has been too great." Laura didn't look happy about it, resignation was a better description.

"I can see that. I can really see that." Abby drummed her fingers on the table. "All right, surrendering to the extreme here. Is there a spell or a seer that would let you know the kind of baby that you were expecting?"

Seesee and Laura now looked to each other and then back to her. "Seers are closely guarded by the council so that they don't burn out. A cross-breeding would not be worthy of assessment."

"Have you asked?"

"Uh, no. We haven't bothered to ask." The blush was obvious in her tone.

"So you are happily unhappy?"

"Yes."

Abby was flabbergasted. "How long can you live like that?"

"Until Verne gives up or dies." Ow. Her voice had gone as cold as the northern oceans.

"Harsh."

"It's a harsh reality. Only the Were representative or the Mer representative to the council can request access to the seers for us." Her face was now carefully blank.

"Am I being sent to the council to report on Miranda's attacks on me?" They both nodded. "Then I may be able to ask some questions for you. Write them down."

Hope crept into Laura's eyes, lighting them from within. She quickly blinked to hide her emotion, but did agree, "Yes. I will give you the questions that you need to ask. If you can get to the seers, it would indebt us to you always."

"Nonsense. You will owe me nothing." It was Abby's turn to look calm and sedate.

"We will owe you a great deal for this favour."

"Nope. You helped me move."

Chapter Thirty-Four

THE VISIT WITH LAURA HAD LEFT HER IN A PENSIVE MOOD. IT WAS only the ring on her doorbell that managed to make her move.

A postal carrier was waiting for her. That in itself was unusual. In her experience, they rang the door and then dropped the pickup slip in her box, never staying to see if she was actually home. She wondered idly if he was breaking some kind of charter by waiting for her.

"Annabeth Hanover?"

He knew the answer, she could see it in his eyes. Friendly eyes, but they saw too much in each glance. Creepy eyes. "Yes."

"I need a signature for this." He extended a parcel to her that was a foot square. It had about seventeen *Fragile* stamps on it and Abby was amazed that it had made it in one piece.

She remembered that the words half-demon had been used in reference to her mail carrier. She tried to meet his eyes as she scribbled her name on the slip. They were a fascinating shade of golden brown that shifted to red when he caught her looking. "Thank you, Nexus. Here is your parcel. The instructions are inside."

As he turned to make his way back to his vehicle, she called out, "Wait!"

"Yes, Ma'am?"

"What's your name?"

"Steven Murdoch, Ma'am." He winked. "Have a nice day." He gave her a little wave and continued on his route.

"What did you expect? Beelzebub Junior? Twit." She kept up her private muttering through the main hall and into the kitchen. As she rested the parcel on the dining room table, she checked out the window to see what the gnomes were up to.

Their happy frolics warmed her heart, but she did have to wonder where they got the chainsaw.

She checked the time and cursed. It was time to enact plan A.

Chapter Thirty-Five

"LAURA? ARE YOU HERE?"

"Come in, Verne. Dive in. I finally decided to take Laura up on her offer of a hot tub soak and got her to lure you here." Abby leaned back in the water and let it churn.

"Why?" He was puzzled. It was obvious. He tilted his head to one side like a dog that just heard a funny noise.

"You and I got off on the wrong foot. This is our chance to clear the air." Her hair was pinned above her ears so she heard the *harumph* that he whispered over the noise of the tub jets.

"I will accept your offer. I keep a suit inside, I need to change."

Abby could bet that he didn't usually wear a suit in this tub, but she appreciated the wild sprint to his home to find one. She was getting better at tracking energy and she had focussed on his while he was standing in front of her.

Xander she could find anywhere. He could be in the seventh circle of Hell and she would still know where he was. Stupid talent.

Slightly out of breath, Verne re-appeared. He was wearing his swim trunks, but they were paired with his t-shirt, socks and sneakers.

"Come on in, wolfman. Time for a chat." Her hand splashed the surface and patted the water lightly.

He was down to only his trunks in no time and easing into the water. "What about?"

He lost his grip on the edge and splashed in when she said, "You and Laura." She let him come to the surface and collect himself.

He leaned back and tried to look nonchalant. "Laura is my mate."

Abby sighed deeply. "Yes. I know that. But do you know why she is keeping you at arm's length instead of trying to see what babies with fur and fish tails look like?"

He blinked at her. He wanted to know, he really did. Asking a stranger was out of the question. "I wouldn't mind hearing your theory."

"Really? That's nice, because that is why we are here."

"Is it?"

"Yes, Commander Obvious."

"Then why is Laura attempting to maintain a distance between us?"

Abby smiled. He finally asked her a question. A good one. "There are several factors. For example, you know that she is a mermaid?"

"Of course I do."

"Then what will you do when she remains young and beautiful while you age?"

"Thank my lucky stars." He smiled.

He actually smiled at her. He had no problem marrying a woman who would outlive him by centuries. "If you had children and they were born as merfolk, how would you feel about them being under water until they learned how to shape shift?"

He blinked slowly. "How long would that take?"

"Anywhere from five to eight years." Based on his shock, Laura and Verne had not yet had this conversation. Idiots.

"As long as I knew where to find them and could dive to visit, I suppose that I would be all right with it." Huh, she hadn't even thought of visitation.

"And if you couldn't visit?"

"Then I would wait until they could join me on the surface."

Abby pondered that, then went back on the attack. "And if your child was born were? Would your society accept it?"

"They have taken in half-bloods before. It is not unknown." He gave it some serious thought, and as he mulled it over, Bitsy brought out some fruit drinks. There was no alcohol in them, just fresh fruit and ice. He gave her a long look and a bow as he delivered the beverages.

"Laura told me that anytime they offer me something with you around, I am to let you drink first from my cup."

"See, she really does love you." Abby grinned brightly and took sips of both beverages. They tasted the same and she handed one to Verne. He took it with a nod of thanks. "Thanks, Bitsy. The tub does get a little warm."

"Do they speak to you?"

"Sure they do, didn't you hear him when he came up? He said that it was to quench our thirst as this tub is rather warm."

"He didn't say anything. His mouth didn't even move." Verne looked concerned for her mental health.

"But I swear I heard him."

"You probably have some connection with your creatures that no one has discovered yet. The Nexus that created creatures did usually live and die alone."

"Ouch. That kind of stings. So I am nuts and I can hear garden gnomes?"

He gave another of his genuine smiles. "In a nutshell. Not the worst thing that could happen to you in this situation."

"I suppose not. Now, for another thing that is keeping you two apart. Me."

He sat up at that. The scowl on his face made her glad that technically he was sworn to protect her.

"Laura was selected by the matriarch of her clan to become part of the…I dunno… Nexus Guard?" She shrugged. It hadn't been explained to her completely either. "She can't leave me to become a mate and if she gets pregnant and it is a merfolk baby, then she will have to leave and return to the sea. That would dishonour her clan and she won't have that."

Stunned did not begin to describe him. "You. She. How did you find out about all this?"

She had a smug smile on her face. "Because I asked her. About your relationship. About social conditions. About why she was here. Things you could have done, you big dummy." He sipped quietly at his drink for a while, chewing on the information she had just flung at him. She leaned back and let the jets pulse and swirl her tension away.

"So what about it? You wouldn't have ambushed me here if you didn't have something in mind."

"You are very astute. I am going to be testifying in front of the council and I want to petition them for a seer vision into your future. I want them to look at all the possibilities."

"And if her children will be mer? What will you do then? She will have to leave and she will not shame her family that way."

"If her children will have tails, then I will petition the mer representative for permission for her to mate and reproduce with you. No shame or dishonour attached. I will ask. If he or she says no, then I will tell you and you can make your plans from there. Include a lot of birth control in those plans by the way. I am just getting used to you guys."

Verne's face actually cracked more than a smile. He chuckled and eventually broke into a full-throated howl. Birds and squirrels ran for cover.

Abby was surprised at his reaction until she realized that she was guaranteeing him that no matter what happened, he had what he wanted. With or without children, Laura would be his.

She had just promised him his fondest wish. What had she gotten herself into?

Chapter Thirty-Six

SHE LET VERNE RETURN TO HIS HOME OR TO GO OUT AND ROMANCE Laura, she had no idea. She was enjoying the play of light on the water of Laura's pool. It was so soothing.

"So you are going to bat for Laura and Verne? Fantastic." Seesee was behind her, but she had felt the gorgon approaching from half a block away.

"Whenever I get sent to the council, I most definitely will. People who know that they are in love and who can maintain that love should be encouraged at any cost. Besides, the worst thing that they can say is no. I have minimal dignity so asking strangers for favours is not a difficult stretch for me. Not when there is a good cause at stake."

"They are definitely a good cause." Seesee looked at her, then out at the water sadly. "I wish that there was an easy fix for me."

"Isn't the mysterious and invisible Miklos your fella?"

"Yes. But I was referring to my inability to have children. When we were little, we were told about the costs of being what we are. I cried for days."

"That only the oldest daughter would have children?"

"Yes. Three little girls, who would grow into three powerful gorgons." She nodded and her hair hissed lightly and caught the breezes. She was quite beautiful as her hair danced in ethereal wind, her skin bronzed by the sun and tears held in her eyes.

"But you wanted your own little baby."

"Just one who would be mine and a man who would love me."

"What about Miklos?"

"He's a vampire. It's part of the reason that I started dating him. He couldn't reproduce if he wanted to. It would take a powerful spell, or an incredible burst of magic to bring him life for even an evening."

"I can manage the magic, but that doesn't solve your problem."

"No, it doesn't. But I suppose until I can figure out something or live without a child."

A thought occurred to Abby and she opened her mouth.

Seesee said, "No, I don't want one of your creatures."

Abby shut her mouth. "Wow, Seesee. You are good."

"I know, but it was pretty obvious where your mind was heading." She touched Abby on the shoulder "The thought was nice, but I don't need a fake child, I need a real one."

It was ironic that Seesee was consoling her. Abby was the one who could bring anything to life that she wanted to, as well as have kids, and she was feeling guilty about not being able to share that with her friend. She wiped the tear from her eye. She was crying where Seesee wouldn't. "Tell me about your sisters."

"My sisters. My sisters. Well, the eldest is Melly, Amellix. She is five years older than me. My other sister is two years older than myself. Her name is Trellatrix, but we call her Tinny. That or butt head. She calls me stink bug."

Abby couldn't contain her giggle. "What about your nieces? Do they all have x's in their names?"

"No, they got away with g's. Gwendolyn, Gennifer and Georgia." A smile came to her face as she thought about them.

"Lemmee guess. You spoil them rotten?"

"Yup. They need all the childhood they can get before their powers emerge."

"When will that be?"

"When they turn twenty. Each of us surrenders our powers in birth order to the next generation. I will miss it, but I have eighteen years before Georgia will be ready."

"I suppose it would be crass to ask if the powers transferred upon death?"

"No. Not at all. But in the modern age, we no longer live together in the same area. It is a nasty surprise to suddenly have your hair attacking the manicurist who cut your cuticle. We engage in a steady and controlled ceremony. Each one is like a wedding and a wake all in one."

"Sounds fancy."

"It is. Very. We buy special dresses, get our nails done, and our hair styled."

"I thought you told me that you got your powers when you were younger?"

"My aunt died. Car accident." Now a tear trickled from Seesee's face. For her lost childhood, her beloved aunt or the shock of the transformation. "We are bonded to the last generation at birth. My sisters got their transfer in ceremony and solemnity. I got mine in a memory of fire and blood."

"Whoa. You got the memory as well?"

"That is why we try to pass it along in a controlled manner. It spares the next generation a certain amount of trauma."

"What if the eldest dies before she can reproduce her three daughters?"

"The ability to bear will pass to the next oldest, with all the power, energy and memories of the first. The first child will get their powers immediately." She stopped and smiled "Well, as soon as they grow hair."

Abby was giggling again. Images of a child trying to use the downy fluff that they were born with to lift a rattle romped through her mind. "Wow. Do you have family photos?"

"Sure. That is part and parcel for being the youngest. I keep the family archive."

"Cool."

Chapter Thirty-Seven

HER GNOMES HAD BEEN SHOPPING.

Someday she was going to get a bill for the supplies. As soon as the home and garden centers figured out where they were going. She felt slightly guilty, but only slightly. The day that they brought home a backhoe, she would worry. And possibly run screaming into the darkness. Until then, as long as they stayed reasonable, she would let them engage in petty theft.

They were gnomes after all. It was in their makeup to take what they needed, she had designed them that way.

She should follow their example. She stood at the window, watching her creatures and thinking about their future. Abby could only hope it was a calmer one than their first week of life. Something caught her attention. There was a sound in her vicinity and it was insistent.

A metallic gong sound was emanating from the box on her dining table. Hmm. To open it or not to open it, that was the question. A frisson of anticipation crept up her spine and a burst of magic with it. What the hell.

The wrapper was plain and brown, no postmark and only her name and address on the top of the parcel. The gong rang again, this time she could feel the reverberations through the box. Closer inspection with her inner eye made her sigh with relief. It had Xander all over it.

Three layers of wrap were shredded in her haste to get to the tiny hand mirror that was making all the noise. It rang again. She picked it up and stared at it. "Hello?"

Xander's familiar features appeared in the tiny reflective surface. "Abby. How are you doing?"

"Fine, I suppose. Is Miranda all checked in?"

"She is. Listen, I am sorry that I didn't spend more time with you last night."

"It's fine." It wasn't fine and they both knew it. She was pissed.

"Even I can figure that one out. I am making my presentation to the council later this afternoon. Can I call you this evening?"

"You mean on this mirror?"

"Sure, they are fantastic. Portable and no roaming charges."

"But what if you don't want to be seen?"

"Ah, but what if you do?"

Oh, he had her there. The things that she could see while talking to him had her vaguely intrigued. His shirt was open, the column of his throat visible and his hair was falling over his left eye in a manner that made her want to push it back. Those golden strands were so tempting. She wanted to pound her forehead on the table. She was so easy when it came to this one particular man. She only wished she knew why. "Fine. What time?" The words were out of her mouth before she knew what was happening.

"Around nine-thirty or so? Is that all right?"

"You are pushing in on my bedtime, Xander."

"I just think I need to explain a few things about me and Miranda."

"Whatever, fine." She let go of the mirror and the surface image of the traitorous hunk next door turned back into a reflective surface. "Jerk" Of course he only wanted to explain his relationship with Miranda. He didn't want to see how Abby was. Bastard.

She was sulking. There was no doubt about it. She even toyed with the thought of trying to get some of the gnomes to eat the Ex-Lax éclairs. That was just wrong. She shook herself and tried to concentrate on local news only to switch the television off when the words, "Mysterious Thefts at local Home and Garden Centers have been linked to thieves dressed as garden gnomes. View security footage after this message."

"Well hell."

Chapter Thirty-Eight

It was embarrassing to be hiding from her own remote control, but she had managed to tuck in far into the back of her refrigerator. She would not be tuning in for views of her babies committing grand theft any time soon.

Mitsy and Harby were currently tidying up from the barbeque that had been used to prepare her dinner. Ruffles was too flammable, Skint was just naked and Splint was tipsy. Her beloved Bitsy was too short to help. Mitsy and Harby both had gloves.

Without the television to entertain her, she was forced to either visit her neighbours or grab her sketchbook. She picked the pencil and paper.

The neighbours had been over enough today. She needed the quiet of her design phase. So design she did. The pencil flew over the page, sweeping in bold strokes and tracing in delicate lines. She couldn't identify what her first sketch had been so she peeled back a page and started again on a new clean white sheet.

This one was much better. She could work out a mouth, teeth, pointed ears. Claws, limbs and wings took up the majority of the design. She had her first flying creature.

Now, should she build it or not? It was quite a conundrum. She would have to sleep on it.

A gong sounded and she winced. Checking her watch let her know that it was indeed nine-thirty. Punctual, he was.

She let the gong sound four times before answering it. She was half hoping that he had given up when she lifted the hand mirror so she could see into it. Once again, it lit up immediately with Xander's face and he looked like he was ready for bed. This was going to be interesting. She settled onto her own bed and propped her torso up with pillows. He was already speaking.

"I wanted to apologize once again for taking off without talking to you first. It was unforgivable."

She couldn't stop herself from sniffing in disdain. "You wanted to make sure your ex was all right. I understand that. I don't have to like it, but I understand it." She was proud of herself for being so calm. The art therapy had worked.

"That wasn't why...damn!" He rubbed at his hair with one hand and the strands tousled in a light and delicate mess. "That wasn't it."

"What was it then? I am very curious." She snuggled deeper into her pillows. The soft surface comforted her almost as well as a stuffed animal would.

"Abby, she tried to kill you."

"I know. I was there."

"Well, her talent didn't stop when she was knocked out. As soon as she came to again, she would be able to do it again." His hand was back in his hair. "She tried to kill me twice on the way to the council. It was only the two guards that were sent to us that stopped her from killing me. Since I was not the driver, it wasn't as bad as it could have been."

"She tried to kill you? While you were in a car with her?"

"A minivan, but yeah. Listen, Miranda and I dated for about six months when I first moved to Oak Point. After that I saw her for the unbalanced being that she was."

"Then why didn't you report her to the council?"

"She had a rough life with her family. I didn't want to queer the deal if it was something that only came out with me in the vicinity."

"But she tried to kill you."

"She wanted to hurt you by killing me."

"It would have done that. I don't know what I feel for you, but your death would have hurt me quite a bit." It was a pale expression of how she felt, but the amount of time that they had spent together didn't warrant the L-word yet. Or she didn't think it did. His smile dazzled her.

"It wasn't a resounding declaration, but I will take it."

She was holding the mirror in her right hand and she began to trace around the edge with her left. Tiny trickles of power leaked into the mirror and suddenly she was seeing a woman with her head thrown back and masculine hands on her breasts. It took a moment for her to realize that she was seeing a memory and that the memory was Xander's.

With a blush heating her face, she jerked her left hand from the mirror. The look in Xander's eyes and the flush on his own skin told her all she needed to know. The memory had been displayed on both mirrors.

"How did you do that?"

The angle of his mirror had changed slightly and she could see the tent of an erection within his trousers. Playing dumb was still an option. "Do what?"

"Put that image on the mirrors that put that blush on your cheeks. And your nose and your forehead. And that made your nipples tent under your t-shirt and bra." He was aroused, but smug.

"Let me think for a minute." So she did. She thought about what she had been imagining when the image appeared. She had been wondering if he was truly attracted to her or if it was just her talents as a Nexus that had him at her door. "I was wondering if you really liked me and why. And then I touched the mirror and a bit of power leaked into it."

He looked more pensive and less horny now. "Could you do that again?"

"What? Wonder about you?"

"Or whatever. Whatever you want to know, think about it and touch the mirror." He was intense.

There was something in his mind and it wasn't naked pictures of her. Dang. What did Seesee's family look like? She stroked the mirror and again felt the almost passive movement of energy. Instantly she saw the picture of three mocha-skinned sisters with hair in a variety of designs and states of excitement, with three little girls who looked like the oldest sister. The little girls were close in age and laughing as the older sisters sat around a table and had tea. Hair was handing the dishes around in typical gorgon fashion and, as they sat there, two men walked into the room, one hugging Seesee's oldest sister and one putting his hands on the shoulders of the middle sister. Seesee was the only one who was alone. Suddenly it was too much for Abby. She jerked her hand from the mirror and soon saw the image of Xander again. "I got my answer. Did you see it?"

"I did. You wanted to know about Seesee's family." He was shaking his head. The mirror bounced lightly as he did. "Amazing. This is a talent that has never been documented in a Nexus."

"Great. I am even more of a freak than I had imagined. Could you leave this out of the documentation?"

"Difference is a good thing."

"I could just be enhancing the existing enchantment that lets us use these silly things as a communication device."

"It is possible. When I get back there, would you be up for experimentation?"

"Sure. If I am not washing my hair that night."

"Ouch. What am I thinking about right now?"

Sighing she ran her finger across the glass only to jerk her hand off as if the glass was hot. The image he had fed her certainly was.

"Aw, you didn't see all of it."

"I saw enough. Didn't you?"

"Not nearly enough." His erection was more than a tent now, it was a pavilion. "See you in a few days, but I will ring you again tomorrow."

"Nine-thirty?"

"Yes. Dress accordingly, I want to play with this new talent of yours." A lascivious wink and he was gone.

The stunned reflection was her own once again. Wow. That had been interesting. And it was slightly more convenient than a web cam. No cables.

The mirror itself puzzled her. Did it only work when it was in use by two parties or could she peek in on other thoughts and families? Wow.

That was too perverse for words. She would not let this bizarre turn of her life turn her into a supernatural peeping tom. Unless she was spying on Xander, but then she would stop at the edge of the stalker limit. She hoped.

Self-control was something that she was still working on.

Chapter Thirty-Nine

Her charge had built up again by the time she woke up. Dreams of a naked Xander spurred on by the images of the night before no doubt had something to do with it.

She tried to ignore it, but the magic pounded and tingled in her brain. It also defied all her attempts to drain it, in the house, the backyard, even the oak tree would not take the power. Something had to be done.

Working from the sketch that she had made the afternoon before, she started to create her newest creature. Perhaps that would get the power out of her and into something else.

Her gnomes tried to help her by bringing her the materials that she had used to create them. The resin, plaster and wire were all well meant, but not for this creature. She shooed the gnomes outside so she could concentrate and went back to her lab...uh, workroom.

This creature was dainty, a conglomeration of wire and silk, stuffing and thread. It had polymer fingernails and black velvet wings. Blue hair spilled down its back and a tiny toga dressed it up a bit.

She was directly sculpting the features in fabric as opposed to the casting method she had used for the gnomes. It needed to stay light, airy and delicate, but it had steel wiring for a skeleton. It would be strong.

The eyes were the final touch. She painted them with acrylics after she had finished the rest of the body. Eyes brought the soul of the creature to life and she couldn't run a needle through it while it was looking at her.

So eyes were always her last step.

In this case, there was one more. Holding the creature between her hands, she let the creative energy flow from her into the bundle of fabric and wire.

"I am good!" Was her first cry and then she was ducking and trying to catch her new creature. Stupid wings.

THE GNOMES TURNED THEIR heads as one to look at the house where the Nexus was at work. Apparently she was happy about something.

They continued to cavort and construct in the backyard, the Nexus needed a new place to meditate and a gazebo with an inlaid floor was the perfect spot. Now they just needed to finish it. Occasionally a swinging board caught one of them by surprise and a fight broke out, but tempers cooled as quickly as they flared and they resumed their task.

An hour after the first outburst and some sharp banging noises were heard emanating from the workroom. The aura of the same creative magic that had brought them to life was pulsing in a wave throughout the house and into the yard.

As one, they turned to bask in the fantastic feel of the animation magic coming from the Nexus. It was warm, loving and oh-so-powerful. And right now their benefactor was cursing a blue streak and shouting.

"Get off the ceiling fan, you little twit."

Curious, the gnomes walked to the patio door to watch the goings on within.

The Nexus was trying to catch their new sibling and that sibling was flying. "Get off the drapes! Ow! Off my head!"

With blatant curiosity, they watched the rapid approach of the new addition. They winced in sympathy as it collided with the clean glass. The Nexus soon got a hold of it and, holding it tightly, she brought it out to meet them.

"BOYS AND GIRLS, THIS is Buffy. She is the gargoyle prototype and my first flying creature. And possibly my last." Abby was proud, irritated and exhausted all at the same time. The sudden takeoff and ensuing chase had taken her by surprise. A tiny chirp from the beastie in her arms made her look down. Buffy was as fascinated by the gnomes as they were by her.

Taking a deep and calming breath, she released the creature from her arms and watched it glide softly to land in front of its peers. Buffy fluffed her long silky hair and extended her clawed hand. One by one, the gnomes took it and engaged in a cordial introduction that smacked of Victorian origins.

"Okay, now that you have introduced yourself, Buffy, I want you to stay in the area. You can fly around Oak Point Way, but not into the town. If people see you, they may get a little scared. Do you understand?" The tiny head with the sparkling eyes and the distended fangs nodded gently. "Then, feel free to fly any time you wish."

With a gleeful shriek, her latest creation took to the skies and headed straight toward the town center.

With a shudder and a long look at her gnomes, she came to the inescapable conclusion. "This is so going to bite me in the ass."

Chapter Forty

AFTER TWO FULL DAYS OF IGNORING WHAT MUST BE GOING ON, she had to know what the news was reporting. Buffy had returned to her home and nested in the oak quite happily. Aside from her trepidation on creating more gargoyles, Abby just couldn't leave Buffy as the only one.

Angel and Firefly were born the day after Buffy returned. Abby smiled every time she looked at them. She was a huge Joss Whedon fan.

She chatted with Xander every evening and he told her absolutely nothing about what was going on. However, she learned that she could indeed tune into his lascivious thoughts at will, while he was on the line, so to speak. Nothing when the mirrors were not engaged.

It was the power generated by those two chats that had brought Angel and Firefly to life.

They nested happily with Buffy, but had an unfortunate tendency to buzz the population of Sargent.

Abby rummaged in her fridge and found the remote behind the pickles. Of course, she could have turned the television on manually, but then what was the point of the remote control?

With a strange combination of excitement and nausea, she took up her position on the couch and only vaguely heard the slide of the patio door. She fumbled slightly, but got the television on and turned to local news.

"In local news, more unidentified creatures have been seen in the town of Sargent, but these ones fly." The anchor was trying to keep a straight face. "Here is footage of the creatures stealing baseball hats and a variety of headgear from people picnicking in the park. The footage was recorded by a local woman who was documenting a Frisbee competition."

The screen changed to a bright sunny day, the first few seconds were nothing but Frisbees flying and being caught. A startled cry off screen made the camerawoman spin and there was Buffy, yanking a baseball cap off a teenage boy. Another shout and a swing of the camera showed Angel and Firefly doing the same. They hovered for a moment, comparing their catches, then flapped off toward home, disappearing into a clump of trees.

"The creatures have not yet been identified by zoological experts at the Winnipeg Zoo, but they seem to be a combination of spider monkey and bat."

A warm body settled on her left shoulder and another on her right. They snuggled against her head, "Oh, no. You are not getting away with it that easily. Why are you stealing baseball caps?"

A large snuffling noise came from the left of her head. "They *smell?* That's why? Oh boy. You are one twisted little pack of critters."

The telly was now showing views of Harby and the crew carefully shopping at three in the morning at the local Home and Garden centre.

"You guys know that I don't have enough money to pay for all the stuff you have stolen, right? And as soon as they figure out where you are coming from, they will be knocking down my door." Warm bodies pressed against her legs and she closed her eyes as the tiny image of Skint watered the plants in his own special fashion before leaving them behind.

Historical pictures now flashed on the screen. These were interesting. "We delved into the origin of this type of occurrence and came up with a few of these events in obscure histories. Gremlins appeared in fiction in 1929, these creatures were never before seen, but are documented as having a particular interest in flying aircraft. They caused mischief on both fronts in World War II." Pictures of grotesque creatures, artist renderings, also moved across the screen.

Abby surmised that is must have been a slow news day.

"Ancient societies also recorded events of this nature. A mass migration of statues from Pompeii to Rome before the Vesuvius explosion. A flock of gargoyles off a variety of churches in the thirteenth century in Germany and a stampede of stone lions and dragons were sighted helping people escape from the Great Fire of London. Is Sargent the next town to add itself to this unusual distinction? After the break, why crossing the street may cause cancer..."

She snapped the off button and glared at her little family. Angel and Firefly were on her shoulders, Buffy was on her left arm and the gnomes were clustered around her on the floor.

"All right, boys and girls. It is time for the facts of life." She made sure that she had all of their attention and kept going, "I can't afford the changes and upgrades that you are making to my yard. I can't afford to be sued for what you are stealing or the people you are freaking out."

The little ring of faces grew sad.

"I do not want you stealing money. If you happen to find it in your travels, buy yourselves some ice cream or something. Do. Not. Take. Anything. That. Isn't. Yours. To. Take. I love what you have done so far. But I only had enough money to buy this house. I didn't have any left over for renovations." A thought occurred to her. "You know, my publisher sounded interested in another book. Maybe I should..." A small hand tapped her on the leg. Her camera was in Splint's hand.

"Buffy, Angel, Firefly, come with me. It's time to earn your keep." She wasn't sure where they would be displayed to their advantage, but she may as well give it a try.

The project that had kept the gnomes out of her house had been one of amazing proportions. They had created a small version of Stonehenge where the explosion had occurred. It was the perfect place to take pictures of the gargoyles.

Taking pictures of moving gargoyles was an event in and of itself.

Acting as her assistants, her light meter, tripod, extra lenses and memory sticks were delivered to her in short order with Harby trying to keep the gargoyles under control. She just wished he hadn't whipped out his tiny handcuffs. What had possessed her to give him handcuffs?

Eventually, the lady of wings agreed to pose in a still fashion as did her consort and companion.

It was almost like photographing a wedding. A really weird wedding. But after hours of posing them, adjusting their minimal clothing and flaring their wings, she was finished. She was ready to craft the book and send it off to see if it would be a good buy for her publisher.

Her gnomes kept her fed and answered the door when Laura showed up. They led her in and sat her down.

"Hiya, Laura." She was on page thirty-two, describing a wrestling match between the muscular Angel and the lighter Firefly. Apparently, it was over the cookie on top of one of the stones.

"Hi, Abby. What are you working on?"

"Another book."

"Oh. What for?"

"To make money. I am going to have to pay off the merchants that have been missing items that are showing up in my yard."

"That is very noble of you, but why don't you ask the council to take care of it?"

"Because I pay my debts and I don't know those fellas."

"Fair enough. What is your book about?"

Harby offered her a cup of tea.

Abby looked up, smiled and took a sip of the scalding brew. "Whoa. That's hot. This new one is called Gargoyles in the Round. It features pictures of my new critters, Angel, Buffy and Firefly."

"Aren't those the names of television shows?"

"Yep. I am a Joss Whedon fan."

"Who?"

"The guy that developed the shows. He does good work."

"Oh." She absorbed that for a moment. "Did you know that your creatures are on the local news?"

"Yup. I saw them. It is what spurred me to want to finish the book. I am responsible for those thefts."

"Great. But did you notice that people are trying to track them?"

"Uh, no. I missed that bit. I thought that Oak Point Way was hidden from the view of people without magic."

"It is. The river isn't. You are featuring with your gargoyles on the Six o'clock News."

"Fuck."

Chapter Forty-One

It wasn't as bad as she had imagined. Sure, she was obviously taking photos of her creatures in the tiny grainy picture. But it merely looked as if she was friendly with the strange creatures. That is, until her gnomes gathered around and started to hand her stuff. Then she knew she was busted.

Her agent called three hours after the news. "Honey, was that actually you? On the news, I mean."

"Yeah, Tina, but I am not outing myself quite yet. If they don't know who I am, I am happy." Her agent only called when she wanted something. "What do you want, Tina?"

"I couldn't help but notice that you were taking photos in that footage. Is there another book in the offing?"

"Yes. Do you want it via email or snail mail?"

"Email please. We can't afford to miss the frenzy that is starting in Sargent. It could be the next Mystical Spot."

She sounded genuinely excited so as they spoke, Abby went to her computer and started to send the enormous book and photo files. "You had better clear out your email, this thing is huge."

"I am ready for it. Send it on through."

A few dozen keystrokes later, "Here it comes. Let me know what you think." She waited while Tina Stephanic muttered and opened the upload.

"Gargoyles in the Round! Fantastic!" Happy chortling noises came from her end of the phone.

"So do you think you can sell it?"

"Honey, I think I already have a bidding war on my hands. This news cast is just what I needed to make my point."

"Doesn't the publisher for Gnomes get first crack at it?"

"Nope. We took it out of their contract when they wouldn't give you the advance that we needed."

"Nice." She smiled. A relaxed smile for the first time in days. Tina would take care of her. Her own money depended on it. It was a fair bargain.

"You leave this with me and I will be back to you in a few days. The first pictures of the gargoyles are going to net us a pretty penny."

The image of Tina rubbing her hands together with anticipatory greed had Abby laughing. "Night, Tina. Enjoy your dreams of money."

"Night, Abby. Think of more creatures to photograph."

"Aye aye, commander. Night." Abby hung up. She sighed deeply. Perhaps selling out her critters wasn't the most horrible thing she could do. And they really didn't seem to mind.

Perhaps she could think of a few more creatures to make. But she was going to let her family settle in for now. Too many new additions would wreck the balance of her family. Nine kids in a month was too much. She was becoming a fan of planned parenthood.

Chapter Forty-Two

To escape the stresses of the news, the gnomes and the gargoyles, not to mention the questions being asked by her neighbours, Abby needed a distraction.

With a bit of time on her hands, she went into her room and took out her big book. Upon careful examination and manipulation, she was able to open it. There was nothing on the pages and she sighed and flipped through the empty book as she imagined what it should have held. Tales of knights and ladies, dragons and fairies. Instead of those stories, this book held nothing.

She sighed and closed the book, drumming her fingers on the surface. A clatter from the kitchen sent a thrill of magic through her and, to her astonishment, the binding of the book answered her power surge. The book glowed, shimmered with a bright magic. Lemon, gold and pink swirled across Abby's inner eye. It was amazing.

Abby's hands trembled as she finally reopened the giant tome. At first she was confused, there was nothing on any of the pages. But she remembered the way that the mirror had worked for her and how the book responded to her so she sent a tiny burst of magic through the book.

It shivered in her hands and words swam to the surface of the page:

If you are reading this, then you are the new Nexus and I hope that this chronicle finds you free and happy. Not all with our talent have been so fortunate. If you are in custody, I hope that this chronicle gives you the key to freedom.

Do not fear for the safety of this book as it lives to protect itself and to come to the Nexus when they begin to master their powers. As there is only one of us at a time, it is only one place at a time. No one who does not generate magic can read it.

I had hoped that after me, each Nexus would add to the book, but perhaps that has not happened. It is with this in mind that I tell you of my life, my capture and my death, for if this book has left my side before I can change this sentence, I have fallen at the hands of my captor. I am hoping that that is not the case.

So I am thinking that I should begin with my story...

Abby almost dropped the book. Holy crap. This was something. She read the next line.

My name is Terranor and I was the Nexus of my time.

With trembling fingers, she punched in Seesee's number. When she picked up, Abby asked her, "What was the name of the first recorded Nexus?"

"Why do you want to know?"

"I just do. Can you get me the name?"

"Sure. Just a minute." Seesee put the phone down on something hard.

Abby could hear the faint opening of the bookcase in the background. The flipping of pages was coming closer to the phone.

"The first one was the only other female that we know of."

"And?"

"Her name was Terranor. Held in the custody of Mervyn Atur. There is no record of her after her twenty-sixth year."

"Thanks." Abby was getting ready to hang up.

"Will you tell me why?"

Abby thought about it. "Eventually. This is a Nexus thing for now."

"Fair enough, have a good night."

"Night." Abby hung up and turned back to the tome in her lap. *My name is Terranor...* This was going to be a long night, but she was eager to start reading of the first of her kind.

My name is Terranor and I was the Nexus of my time.

I didn't know what I was, nor did my mother or father. We lived happily in a small village and my father made a tidy living as a scribe.

May I say at this point that my parents were in love. They delighted in telling me of their first meeting, my father, new in the village, and my mother, working for her father in the tavern. When she saw him, she dumped a tankard of ale into the lap of the man she was serving. He was laughing so hard that he walked into one of the support beams and so was one of the greatest loves I have ever seen born.

Against common practice, my father taught me to read and write. From an early age, I had a love of letters and my parents encouraged learning. Every book that my father copied was given to me to read after the work was completed. I looked for errors and helped him complete the details of embossing and finishing his work.

I was happy there, but when I turned sixteen, something changed. A magus came to our village and examined all the villagers under seventeen. When he looked at me, his eyes lit up and he immediately offered to buy me from my parents.

They were offended by the offer. They were going to wait until I had made a love match before allowing me to leave their home. I had never felt so grateful to have parents who loved me and held my happiness beyond their own, for the magus offered them much gold for me.

The mage left and we thought it was the end of it, but then he returned six months later with an army. He destroyed the village, killed my parents and took me as the spoils of war.

So began my trip into the world of magic, in tears and blood.

Abby gasped as she pulled her mind from the pages of the book. She felt Terranor's grief as her own. A tiny hand put a tissue in her fist and she blinked tearfully at Bitsy. "Thanks."

"You are welcome, Nexus. Would you care for some dinner?"

His lips barely moved, but she heard the words clearly. "Sure. What is on the menu?"

"Caesar salad, chicken fingers and macaroni and cheese. Your favourites." He led the way to the kitchen and waited to hold out her chair for her to be seated.

"I still don't know how you guys all ended up with manners. I had always imagined gnomes as wild and impish." As she sat, Ruffles brought her salad out. "And your grasp of modern sedatives is just amazing."

"Why, thank you. We are what you wanted for us, smart, quick witted and we love the internet."

She paused, her fork half way to her mouth. "You aren't kidding, are you? You guys are cruising the net?"

"We are. It is the most efficient way for us to get information. We can't ask you everything. If we chased you around asking *why* and *what* all the time, you would take your magic back."

She absorbed that and shrugged, then mumbled around her salad, "The magic is yours now, you have made it your own. I could take it back, but it would cost me more than I gained. I love you little guys."

The kitchen ceased all background activities. Abby looked up to see all of her gnomes looking at her with reciprocal affection in their eyes. "I mean it. I wouldn't even be around if you guys hadn't stopped me from driving the great exploding car or if you hadn't shown Xander where the bomb was, it could have gone off at any time. Really. I love you because you are friends, you don't have to stay, but you do. It is the best kind of friendship."

Dang. Now they were all crying. She felt her self engulfed in a seven-way hug with tiny arms and limbs once again. After what she had read, it was a welcome comfort.

I cried for days. It took two weeks of a brutal ride on horseback to reach the magus' home. I was immediately rushed to a set of rooms grander than anything I had ever been in before, but still. I mourned the fifty souls killed to take me prisoner. Each day I prayed, cried and railed against the mad man who had taken me from my home.

It took two weeks for one of the maids to get me to bathe and with my mind numbed by grief and exhaustion I fell asleep in the bathing chamber.

When I woke, the magus was standing over me. He told me that I was a Nexus and that he had to train me. My parents' interference could not stop my destiny, I would become the conduit of magic. Whether I willed it or no.

If the water hadn't been cloudy with soap, I would have been mortified, but I was decently covered until he left. Then I scrambled out of the tub and into a gown that one of the maids held out for me.

I trembled for days.

I had no interest in my destiny, I wanted my family back.

Damned right. Arrogant prick. How dare he take her from her home just so that he could keep her power for himself? Abby was furious on Terranor's behalf. If that magus was here, she would kick him in the balls. Twice. With steel toed boots that had been heated in a fire.

Bastard.

Chapter Forty-Three

MY EDUCATION IN THE MAGICAL ARTS BEGAN AT THE FULL MOON. I WAS taught the history of magic and the first stirrings of my talent began to show. It was when I was folding a doll together out of leaves that had blown in through the window. I had cradled her in my hand and concentrated all my love on her so that I would be able to release her to the winds in prayer for the souls of my parents. The little doll sat up and hugged one of my fingers.

I almost screamed, but at the same time I was fascinated with my creation. She shifted and changed under my watchful gaze until she was the perfect image of my mother. I placed her carefully on my desk and ran to get her one of my handkerchiefs to wear as a dress.

She dressed herself and smiled at me. I smiled back. I had made a friend.

I named her Terza, after my grandmother.

She became my constant companion. She hid in my hair when I had to meet with the magus for my lessons. After a few weeks, she began to speak. Tiny whispers in my ear, but I could understand her. It was just fortunate that others could not. She had very few complimentary things to say about my maids. One was the magus' leman, the other his bastard daughter. Neither was happy to be waiting on a village girl with some as yet unknown talent.

I suppose they thought I was going to interfere with their lord's affections. I wish that they were wrong, but more of that later.

"He wouldn't! Not with all that power flying around." Abby was seething. Xander had been cautious with messing around with her for exactly that reason. What kind of an idiot was this guy?

A cup of hot chocolate was pushed into her hand. Mitsy had carried it between her gloves and was watching Abby carefully. One of her creatures had turned on her reading lamp and placed a shawl around her shoulders. She hadn't even known she had a shawl.

It took months of training, but I finally grasped at what the magus wanted. Enchanted weaponry. He had me start on daggers and then slowly moved into larger items. This concerned me. At no time did he have me pour magic into a shield or even armour. He was going on the attack, but each item exhausted me.

The work was steady, but eventually I began to fail. My hands shook, arms trembled and I began to faint after each outpouring of magic. The magus had no choice but to let me rest. I was taken from his citadel and brought to a country estate, deep in the woods. Terza and I loved it.

Each day dawned bright and clear, even if it was storming outside. The guards brought me every thing I asked for and so I began to ask for materials to create more little beings.

Terza posed for the new little statues that I made out of sticks, yarn, and leaves. I had always bemoaned not giving her wings so that was the first thing I added. After a few fairies flew from my hands, I learned to make them as close to what I wanted before I poured the magic in. It was easier.

Each time I sent the magic into them, I felt a spill of joy through me. It was only when fifty or more of the creatures were flitting about that I recognized the emotion as coming from them. My strength returned and my health.

Hagatha was the maid that was now my companion in exile, but she had an interest in one of the guards that kept her occupied much of the time. She was the one who had to tell me that I had been commanded to return to the house of Lord Magus Mervyn Atur. I cried for the loss of my fairies, but rejoiced that they would remain free in the forest. I sent them deep into the woods where the guards would not see them and got back on my horse to return to my monitored captivity.

I hated him so much.

To my surprise, the situation had changed. Someone had told a council of some sort of my existence and they demanded to have a say in my works. It had taken them two years, but now they wanted to watch what I could do.

"Yeah, I bet they did. Greedy bastards." Abby blinked as her hot chocolate was refilled, she took a deep breath and a deeper sip. Oh, the gnomes had found her stash of Mexican hot chocolate. It was sweet, hot, cinnamon and chocolate. Delicious. Just the thing to calm her before she turned the light bulb into a floating ball of light.

I attended my first ball that night. The council members were elves and merfolk. They danced as if they were lighter than air. I wished that I had half the grace that they exhibited on that night. I still do to this day.

They dipped and swirled, spun and bowed, all to the most delicate music I have ever heard. When one of the men turned to me and asked me to dance, I blushed and confessed that I had never learned.

He told me that now was as good a time as any, that he was an excellent teacher and led me to the floor. I do not remember the dance, but I remember that every time our hands touched, an energy ran from his body to mine. It was magic, but magic that he was giving me. The knowledge of the dance and the ability to move with the music. It was heady. Beautiful.

It was the night I fell in love.

Each pass of our hands, each time I looked into his deep blue eyes, I knew that this was the one I was meant to find. This was the man that made me whole.

When the dance ended, he kissed my hand and I felt it right down to my toes. I returned to my place at the head table and studiously ignored the magus as he glared at me, then the elf, in turn.

I didn't even learn my love's name until the following day. Strykr Elofwel, curator of the council library. He lived for books and knowledge. He was my perfect match.

The magus knew it, too.

The instant that the council members took up residence, he pressed his suit, gifts of ribbon, fabric and sweets came in a constant stream to my quarters. I rejected them all.

My maids and I were allowed to walk in the gardens, with an escort of course. It was on one such excursion that Strykr joined us. He took my arm and asked me how I was treated. I told him that I had clothing and shelter.

He asked me, "What about love?"

I told him that love had died with my family. He nodded as if he understood.

He fascinated me. I had heard of elves in our area, but never seen one up close. The delicate points of his ears held his hair back—the blond waves tumbled almost to his hips. His lips were well sculpted and surprisingly full and sent a blush running through me when he caught me staring. Those blue eyes crinkled up at the corners.

I love his beauty so much. He makes me feel like a princess when he looks at me.

I love that feeling.

I wish it could last forever.

Chapter Forty-Four

Wow. This was intense. Abby was hoping for the couple, even though they were centuries dead by now. It still didn't make it easier to read the pain and confusion that Terranor had gone through. She got up and stretched, working kinks out of her shoulders.

She wished that Xander was here, wished that he hadn't gone back to his house to tidy up after the Miranda disaster. But if he was here, she wouldn't be reading this book. They would probably be curled up on her bed together.

She couldn't know where her life as a Nexus was going, if she didn't know where others of her kind had been. She took a deep breath and jumped back into the emotional turmoil.

There were guards, my maids and everyone was watching as he leaned down to give me my first kiss. I didn't know why he was doing it, I just didn't want him to stop. He had no choice as the magus chose that moment to come around the corner and Strykr was thrown back by a blast of magic so powerful that my hair stood on end.

A member of the council's party rushed to him and started the process of healing the large smoking hole in Strykr's back.

It was an error in judgement on the magus' part. The merfolk held him as he spewed venom for all to hear. I was his, no one was to touch me, he had murdered for me fair and square.

The elves were horrified and I was immediately removed to one of their deep forest villages. I held Strykr's hand every time he was awake enough to ask for me. The damage to his back was so severe that the healer told me he might never walk again. I knew that it wasn't so and when there was a group of healers convening in the elven village, I broke in and asked what they needed to heal him completely.

They answered me. Power. Magic. It was all that they needed, but none of them could reach beyond their limits to complete the healing. I offered them all the power that they wanted and they agreed, more humouring me than anything else I think.

They were rather surprised when I provided enough energy to power them all. It was my worry over Strykr, I think. He was the first creature to offer me kindness since the day I was taken from my village. Well, him and Terza.

His bones and flesh knit in two days. At that point, I firmly had the attention of the village leaders and council representatives. I explained what I had been told by the magus and demonstrated a few things that he had taught me to do. When I mentioned the weapons, they finally began to look concerned. It was about time.

It was obvious that the magus was preparing for a magical war. I told them that he had no defensive weaponry and that I would be willing to provide them with a defence. They seemed pleased.

When Strykr recovered, he began courting me and I am happy to say that he proposed marriage. I found myself heavily in love. The elves held a lovely ceremony for us as we bound our lives together in front of witnesses.

"You go, girl." A trill of happiness went through Abby. In fact, as she read the book, she felt everything that Terranor must have felt. The fear, the hate, the first blush of love and the joy of being with the man she loved. This book was truly magic.

I will spare you the details of our coming together, but it was more than I had ever imagined two people could have. We were two halves of a whole and each day brought us closer to becoming one.

The brief flare of happiness was extinguished when I became with child. The magus had told all who would listen that I was a mule, unable to bear. When I shared my happy news with Strykr, he grew pale, then shook his head and grinned. The pallor he had exhibited was due to the reaction of the elven council in the village.

They would not have a Halfling in their village. We were told to leave. Apparently, the only reason that they allowed Strykr to mate with me was that they expected him to make a more suitable match after I was dead. Since I was supposed to be sterile, there were to have been no offspring to be concerned about.

I looked to my beloved and he put his arm around me. As one we left the village and did not look back. My powers gained strength with my pregnancy and, when we found another elvish village, we offered our skills as a package to them in return for shelter and a place for our young. The offer was accepted and we became citizens of Dath Mor.

That was the village where our first daughter was born. Elspeth. Over the course of the next five years, three more came to join our family, Aolin, Maylal, and Seleeth. Strykr named them all, and never ceased to show his love for me everyday, it was why we had so many children.

Secure in his love, I began to enchant weapons for defence and attack. Three villages banded together to create a masterwork of steel and had it enchanted by me. It was a large sword and they named it Hex-Ca-Libre. The instant that magic flowed into it, I knew that it had a great destiny.

Chapter Forty-Five

"Holy crap. She made Excalibur. Well, enchanted it." Abby was talking to her short and sleepy eyed audience. Gnomes were sitting on every inch of her desk, but left a wide margin around the book. She hadn't realized it, but since her throat felt hoarse, she must have been reading out loud. The gargoyles were perched on the back of a nearby chair and listening raptly. Yup, that settled it, she had been talking. "Shall I continue?" At the entire group of nods, she laughed and then went back to Terranor's happy ending.

Other villages started to come to me for magic. It confused me until one of the elders explained it to me. There is a finite amount of magic in the world at any given time. It resided in people, trees, water and earth. Any one of these can over draw magic. Especially the human magi. They drew on not only their powers, which were considerable, but drained it from others. Usually other races to forward their own agendas.

I was born to replace lost magic, through waste and greed. The earth magic created me to draw on the energy that binds magic between worlds. Those were the purposes of the magus' first lessons, to have me break the wall between worlds and draw power through. Like a fool, I did it.

Once the veil was broken, the power flowed like water, the more I used it, the more I could identify the type and purpose for the magic drawn through. It was good to keep busy, but with four girls, I was so busy that I could almost not see the disaster that was right around the corner.

Rumours came to us at first. The magus was making war and stealing the power of the elven villages. No one could believe it, but I knew that this was exactly what he had wanted. I went to the village elders and spoke to them about the magus. They decided to take a wait-and-see attitude toward the situation.

I prepared for war.

With my children, I crafted tiny warriors, and then not so tiny ones with multiple arms to wield weaponry. Elspeth named them brownies after the mud that we made them from. I whispered my instructions to them and sent them into the forest.

My children brought me pebbles, which I had Strykr enchant into wardstones. The little ones deposited them around the village. They helped me make the village as safe as it could be with no one preparing except our family.

My husband was preparing his own surprise for me. For two years, he worked on creating this book, making it as sturdy as he could for just this purpose. It would not be destroyed by time, wind, weather or fire. His enchantments were powered by our intimate time together, but when he presented me with this tome, I cried.

My father would have loved to have created a book half as beautiful.

My heart wept with both pleasure and pain of remembered loss, but eventually I calmed myself enough to assure Strykr that I loved his gift and that he had not insulted me. Foolish male.

My little Elspeth got excited when she saw the book. She screamed, "That's it, that's it," over and over again. When I finally calmed her, she told me that the book would bring us help.

My eldest was born a seer. The gift woke in her on her third birthday and since then she has had a hard time explaining to us what her magic is telling her. My other daughters are also waking to the gift of foresight, but none as strong as my eldest.

She could not keep away from this tome. She kept stroking it as if to bring it to life.

We received notice that the magus was approaching. He would not harm the village if I was handed over to him. The council met and refused his request. I had become part of them, you see. Half of the elves evacuated the village, but the rest stayed to defend their lands. I provided what help I could, but since I had never completed my training, I could not give enough to the defenders. It has frustrated me.

Elspeth remained fascinated with the book and it was at her urging that I began to pour some magic into it. When the news came that the army was only one day away, I began to write this chronicle so that someone would know of my life and the circumstances of my existence. The next Nexus needs to know the danger that they are in.

I can only hope that my efforts have been successful.

The tale ended there. No other writing swam to the surface and Abby almost screamed in frustration. Dawn had lit her study and her creatures were just as irritated as she was. "What the hell happened?" Her hands were on the phone before she had a conscious thought. "Seesee. I need to know everything about the first Nexus and I need to know it now."

"I thought you might ask for it, I had the archive fax it over last night. I will bring it over right away."

The line disconnected and Abby was left shaking and burning with the need to do *something*. The gnomes had scattered and were busy assembling something that Abby couldn't identify. It involved a large mirror and jumper cables so she didn't want to look too closely. She was pacing by the time Seesee arrived and snatched the documents from her hands with a curt, "Thanks."

"You know, you could tell me what this is all about. I may be able to help." Her hair writhed in confusion.

It was hypnotic to watch, but Abby only spared her a glance before sitting down and reading the history of Terranor. "Sorry Seesee, it's a Nexus thing."

The gnomes shooed Seesee out, much to her consternation. She was trying to say something when they closed the door in her face.

It was a short history. Lord Magus Mervyn Atur took the orphaned Nexus into his charge and trained her as best he could. The ungrateful wretch ran from him and hid with a village of elves. The elves staged a violent revolt against the magical council, which was squelched by the Lord Magus and ended with the elven village and the first Nexus completely disappearing. They were presumed dead. No trace of the village remained after the battle was completed.

Mervyn took pride in his eradication of the elves, although a head count of the dead and a confirmation of the death of the Nexus was never provided. It was all the convincing that Abby needed.

Abby called Xander's cell and left a message. "I am going to be out of touch for a few days. I have something that I have to help a friend with." She knew that she had to move fast. The image of what she needed to do burned in her mind.

The book had given the image to her as it had the image of the gnomes. She would be a fool to ignore it. She was not a fool. Well, not anymore.

Harby tugged on her leg to draw her attention and she looked at what they had made. It was a portal. Sort of. The mirror that Xander had given her was hooked up to her large mirror and two jumper cables lay open for connection.

The marks that she had noted on the Chronicle lined up perfectly with the clips on the cables. As soon as she had the cables in place, she took a deep breath. "I can't believe I am going to try this."

"Neither can I. You are not going anywhere without me." Seesee was back and ready to rumble.

Her hair was a little twisted and Abby figured that she must have picked the lock with it. "Seesee, you can't come with me."

"You are going into the past? To help the first Nexus and her village?"

"Sort of. There will be no village when I am done."

"The history of the gorgons tells the tale of one of us who came from the future for three days. No one has done it yet and yet several have tried. I get the feeling that I am that one. Besides, I am your bodyguard for the week. Until Alexander gets back, I am all you have."

The gnomes were on point, just waiting for Abby's decision. "I guess the more the merrier."

"More? You are taking the gnomes?"

"Bitsy isn't well enough to be on his own yet and having me in the past may affect their power supply. I want to make sure they stay up and running until I get back here." Her creatures looked up at her gratefully. They didn't need to be grateful. She would always protect her critters with everything in her.

"So how are we going to do this?"

"I am going to stretch the magic around the book and create a time bubble that will link us to Terranor. Then I will run my power through the book, hopefully making a connection between her time and ours. Then we pray." Abby bent and put a hand on the Chronicle, starting the process. "I would get closer if I were you. Only items in the bubble are going to make it through the portal."

"Book? What book?" Seesee Montrose barely got the words out before it all started.

Chapter Forty-Six

"Ow. Ow. Ow. Ow. Fucking ow." Every time a small hand touched her face she winced. "Am I going to die?"

"You had better not. If you do, I couldn't kill you."

Hands pushed and pulled her upright and she was surrounded by her creatures and a scowling Seesee.

Her hair was rubbing at her temples and she looked pissed. "Did you know that it would hurt that much?"

"No, or I would have packed some aspirin." Buffy dropped something on Abby's lap and she looked at it curiously. It was an apple. "Thanks, hon." She bit through the sweet crunchy flesh and sighed as the juice flowed down her throat. Her headache disappeared in an instant. Seesee was also munching one and she smiled with relief as her pain eased as well. "You know, you guys are way smarter than I gave you credit for. How did you get so smart?"

"You told us, too. We heard it in the whispers of the magic when we came to life. It has been teaching us since the day you made us." Bitsy gave her that bit of information with a small pat to her knee.

"Okay, kids, where are we?" Slowly, Abby stood and surveyed their surroundings. There was no sign of civilized life, only the endless expanse of forest in front, behind and around them.

"You are standing in the middle of the hunting ground." An elf moved out from behind a tree.

Abby was gob smacked. He looked like Xander. "Who are you?" She was trespassing, but she still couldn't help herself.

"I am Strykr. You are?"

She was stunned. It had worked. They were in Terranor's time. "Pleased to meet you. Can I see your wife, please?" He looked almost angry until she started to pull her power around her. The gnomes stood in front of her and the gargoyles hovered at her back. She turned slightly and nodded to Seesee who let her hair whip wildly through the soft air of the forest.

He stood facing them, scowling protectively at the mention of his mate. "Who are you to ask for her?"

Abby pulled power from the rock and trees, swirling the magic into bright waves. "I am a Nexus and I am here to help. I know all about your wife and courtship and I will prove what I know if you will come here so that I may tell you the name of your wife's constant companion."

His interest was now fully peaked and his eyes grew brighter than she could imagine. Slowly and carefully, she moved toward him with her hands outstretched, her crew hanging behind at a safe distance. She stopped in front of him and waved for him to bend toward her. He did and she whispered the name in his pointed ear, "Terza."

He straightened abruptly and gave her a terse, "Come with me."

Shrugging, she and her entourage followed.

The village was quiet. The few elves that she saw looked at the motley crew that they were and turned back to their tasks. It was obvious that they prepared for war.

Abby could feel the hum of the magic that Terranor was putting out, hell, she could *see* it. The colours of lemonade, pink, lemon and gold were on everything metallic and all doors. She had really tried hard to keep the village safe from the coming invaders.

He paused in front of a home that was surrounded by flowers.

Abby looked through her other sight and saw them glowing softly in the afternoon. Magic blooms.

"Here she is. I will take our children so that you may talk."

"May my gnomes accompany you?"

"Certainly, I think the children will enjoy it."

His lips twitched in a sideways smile that had her heart pounding in her chest. He was so much like Xander it was scary.

He swung the door open and called out as he went inside. "Ladies, we have guests. If everyone smaller than my waist will come with me, it will let the adults speak."

Abby staggered as she walked into the cosy home. A short blonde elfin girl who looked just like her daddy, was clinging to her thigh.

"You came! I didn't think you would, but you did! I saw you!" Tears were in the bright blue eyes.

"Hello, Elspeth. It is nice to meet you. If you hadn't told your mommy about me, I would never have come." She stroked the silky hair gently and gave the little mite a tiny kiss on the forehead.

"So it did work. Strykr told me it would, but I didn't believe him."

Abby was puzzled for a moment until she put it all together. "Your daughters are very like you, aren't they?" She was looking at the only male in the room, aside from the gnomes.

He blushed a bright red. "They share my gifts, yes."

"And you gave her the book."

"Yes."

"And she wrote in the book."

He was almost squirming now. "Yes. I have had the seer's gift since I was a child. I knew Terranor as mine the instant that I saw her. I brought you here knowing what you would do, but not how you would achieve it. I do not have precision in my sight."

She looked over at Terranor, a very unprepossessing woman who was making a small doll on the table. "I think you did a helluva job, Strykr. The knowledge of how to come through time was given to the gnomes when they came alive. I only had a vague idea of what they were building. Now, can you leave us alone? We have Nexus stuff to discuss."

With moaning and protests to stay, the girls, gnomes and elf were shooed out of the house, leaving two Nexus' and a gorgon.

"Welcome. I have to say, I did not have my husband's faith in the magic I put in the book. Welcome."

Tears were in her eyes and Abby moved to hug her quickly. She knew all too well the feeling of being overwhelmed by events beyond her control. She snivelled a little as well. When they finally separated, she said, "My name is Abby, by the way, this is Seesee. We are here to help."

"What can we do?" It was a harsh wail. "They will be here in less than a day and we have no defences in place."

"Terranor, can I call you Terra...we are going to make this village disappear." To say her host's jaw dropped would have been an exaggeration, but she did notice a distinct slackening. "I am serious. We will throw a shield around the village that will keep the invaders from seeing it."

"The magus knows my power, he will see it."

"Well, he would if he could see it. He won't"

"How will you keep it from him?"

"It's a surprise. Call in the short squad, we need some rocks."

"The what?"

"Your kids and my gnomes. We need some rocks. And some clay, mud, sticks, a fire and a few really big branches of poison ivy." She ticked the ingredients off on her fingers, then remembered something. "Oh, and call in your pixies, they can help."

"My what?"

"Pixies. The small fairies that are winged Terzas."

"Oh. How do I do that?"

Abby blinked. She had instincts for her magic. It had never occurred to her that her counterpart would not. "Sit quietly, look with eyes that don't see the world around you and look for your colours."

"Colours?"

"Your magic is coloured by your personality. It is bright, light, yellow and pink." She looked over at the first of her kind and sighed. "Shall I do it?"

"You can call them?"

"I don't see why not. Magic is magic, if I make it tempting enough, they will come."

"May I watch?"

"Sure, but get the little ones busy. We need those supplies."

"Why?"

"We are making brownies." Abby looked over at Seesee while they waited for the kids to be given their tasks. Shrieks of glee reached them.

Just before Terra came back in, Seesee asked, "Do you know what you are doing?"

"I really hope so because this is going to hurt. A lot."

Terra nodded. "They are gathering the supplies. The potter left so we can use her kiln and the clay in her stores."

"Excellent. First the pixies." She sat comfortably in the second largest chair in the room and then closed her eyes almost completely. She sent her senses out looking for magic, dodging what was obviously the magus with his army and continuing until she saw the small flickering lights in the forest. She used her senses to touch those lights one at a time.

They were bright, curious and only to happy to help. They were on their way.

Her eyes opened to a fascinated Terranor staring at her.

"I saw them. They are coming."

"I didn't even feel you along with me. You learn fast." She stood and stretched. "Now. Time for sculpting. To the pottery."

Once she explained the principle, Terranor and her family took over.

The application of the poisoned ivy was left to Seesee's hair. She tucked it into a crevice on each and every hideous creature. "Okay people, don't touch them now. The only one who can get them up and running now is you, Terra."

"Me? Why not you? You have such a grasp of the power."

"Because these are your guardians. No one can grab them and they can cause and create so much havoc that you will be amazed. They will live outside the village and they will thrive. I guarantee you. That and, of course I am going to be back in my time and they will not be able to draw power from me if they need it."

"Oh. I see." The look said she didn't see.

"Terranor, how do you usually draw in power?"

"Uh, well. Not in front of the children."

The little girls giggled.

It was enough to give Abby the last clue. Apparently, power was generated the same way here as back home. "I understand. So why don't you and your husband have a short...conversation, while I keep the kids occupied." Abby winked and waved her off. The gnomes were still capering with the children and Terranor needed a fast energy boost. Only sex or heavy petting was going to be enough. The first Nexus was bemused, but followed her orders and, in thirty minutes, the power shot was out. The wave of magic caressed their sculptures, but it was when Terra returned, patting her hair smooth again, that the brownies came to life.

"Missy? Where do you want us, Missy?" They chirped up as one. Terranor looked surprised as the brownies stood and unfolded their multiple arms and legs.

"You can guard Missy best from the outskirts of the village. Make sure no one breaks the circle of rocks." Abby gave the direction as Terranor was still obviously shocked at how simple the activation was.

"Yes, Missy-friend. We go." Wave after wave of the slender creatures ran past them to take up their positions as guardians. Phase one of her plan was complete.

Chapter Forty-Seven

PHASE TWO CONSISTED OF SHORING UP THE PEBBLES AND KEEPING the barrier seamless. For this, Abby used her magic to charge them, simply dragging her hands through a vat of gravel. The gnomes dug a small trough around the village and laid the bits of gravel in it with astonishing attention to detail.

Abby and Terranor were washing their hands by the village well.

Terra asked her, "Are they your creatures? Did you make them?"

"I did and they are. They are great."

"They seem terribly intelligent."

"They are."

"How do you control them? They seem so loyal."

"What? Control them? I just let them do their thing. They choose to stay with me." She looked over at them and watched them carefully, knowing that her face was showing maternal pride. She couldn't help it, she was proud of all that they accomplished.

"So the pixies as you call them? They will be loyal to me?"

"Probably. It depends on if you were feeling lonely when you created them."

"Very."

"Then, when they arrive, there will be nothing that will stop them from protecting you."

"That is amazing."

"The really amazing thing, to me, is that we came through time and still manage to get ourselves understood. I guess it helps that we were wrapped in your magic when we did." She looked down at herself. "Sorry about the clothing. I didn't have time to find something more appropriate to this time."

"No worries there. The elves often wear rather risqué clothing, it doesn't matter."

"Speaking of the elves, why have none of them offered to help in our little escapade?"

"They leave human matters to the humans. The elves who are here are prepared to die."

"But they don't want to, right? Because if they have a suicide wish they had better hit the bricks. There will be no deaths in this village." The look she got was admiring.

"You are sure about that. I can tell. What do you know of the future?"

"All I know is that the village disappeared, with no reports of deaths or capture. I know how to make that happen."

"How?"

"It's a surprise. I don't mean it to be mysterious, but until we are facing the magus and tell him off, it will not be a reality." Abby shuddered and took a deep breath. "We have to do that before anything else."

"Why? I don't know if I can face him after all these years."

"Because that is the way it was written so that is the way it must be." The words came out of her mouth without a second thought. Abby blinked and rummaged through her brain for the origin of that comment and found nothing. Not even a stray peanut. Something was weird. She muttered to herself, "Shake it off, Abby," and earned a long look from Terranor.

"What is it Abby? You are thinking something. Something important."

"I can't help but feel that something has been pushing me to this point. Even a month ago, I would never have dreamed that magic could throw a person through time. If the gnomes hadn't known what to do, I would have been stuck."

"Well, so far I have not put the knowledge of the portal generator into the book. Where do you think this influence is coming from?"

"I have no idea. I only know that it is unsettling to feel like something is pushing and pulling me to be certain places at certain times." She shook her head again, trying to clear it.

"I am sure that all will be revealed in good time. I can only be grateful that something is pushing you to be here with us at this time." Her skirts rustled as she washed her hands and she had no sooner set the table than an elf came through the door with a tray of food. "Thank you, Anwyn. It is most appreciated."

"You are welcome, my friend. We hope that you have success in these endeavours. In fact, we are depending on it."

The grace that the blonde elf used in the curtsy to Abby freaked her out. It was the manoeuvre of a butterfly, dipping and rising with boneless grace. "Anwyn, may I ask you a question?"

"Of course, my lady." She dipped again with that ethereal grace.

"Could you ask the villagers a question? Could you ask them if they would mind being taken out of the living world?" At the woman's frightened look, she struggled to find the proper words. "I mean. Oh. Hell. I suppose I will have to tell everyone or they won't have the chance to agree or not." Abby squirmed in the seat. Public speaking was not her forté. "I don't have the words now, but if you can arrange a meeting with the members of the village, I would be very grateful."

"I will see to it, Lady." She almost ran from the cottage.

Seesee took that moment to assert herself, "Well *that* went well. Why don't you just tell them that you have invented a plague. It will scare them faster."

"I blew it. I suck at confrontation. Well, aside from when I blew up Miranda, but that was just luck."

Terranor smiled and put the food on the table. "The same luck that has sent you here and created guardians for my village? Good luck, I say."

The gorgon turned to her friend and said, "Tell me what needs to be said. I will tell them at the meeting. I am quite the excellent public speaker."

"Are you sure?"

"There has to be a reason that I am here. This must be it." She smiled and her hair snapped and curled with excitement. "It is either that or to teach these elves the benefits of good pastry. I can't decide."

Abby hugged her friend with relief. "Thanks. I always want to hurl when I am at a podium."

"All right. Abby. Tell me your plan."

Terranor leaned forward as her family trooped in and waved them to silence. She wanted to hear the plan that would remove the threat of the magus from her family. As the Nexus Abby spoke, she felt her eyes widen in surprise.

"It all started when I remembered the *boom*..."

Chapter Forty-Eight

"SO, GOOD PEOPLE OF THE VILLAGE, WILL YOU STAY, KNOWING what will become of you, your children and your grandchildren?"

"We will. The option to seek mates outside the village is appealing. If necessary, we will hold a lottery so that only one is out of the village at a time."

"That will be fair. But the Nexus Abby has another question to put to you. Will you answer her?"

"Of course we will. She has given us this opportunity. We will listen to what she has to say."

Trembling with fear of public humiliation, Abby faced the group of ridiculously handsome elves. "Elders, have you heard of the magical council?"

"Yes. Of course. Several of us are members."

"Then have you heard of the Eternal Archive?"

Brynwyn, the elder, answered, "No. What is it?"

"It is something that exists in my time, an eternal record of all the varieties of magic. Including my own and that of Terranor. Someone needs to keep these records. They need to record the books that have the best spells, the best teachers of each generation and the greatest loves. Would you, this village, become that Eternal Archive?"

"Keepers of knowledge. Keepers of Magical history?"

"Indeed. That is the idea." Abby smiled as the faces around her took on a new glow, the glow of hope. "Before our plan is in action, you must have notified the council of it, I would get to it, if I were you."

Brynwyn craned his neck to the sky.

Abby saw the spiralling bolt of power that he sent out.

"The answer should be back presently."

"I don't know how to measure time here. What is presently?"

A bright glow centred over the communal fire, it swirled and grew by leaps and bounds. Finally a figure stepped from it.

"What nonsense is this that you spread? A disappearing village and a lost Nexus?"

"We need to bring these things to come, Lady Myfir. Tomorrow Mervyn Atur will be here and we will die at his hand unless these things come to pass."

"I just needed to hear it from you lips, Brynwyn. You have our blessing to keep the records and your village shall be charged with gathering knowledge in its quest. Will that suffice?"

"More than you could ever know. Thank you."

"Yes, thank you." Abby should have kept her mouth shut. The fiery creature turned to her. "And what have you to do with it?"

"I am the other Nexus. The one who will return through time." She curtsied back and was quite pleased, considering that she was wearing jeans.

"Then make sure that all progresses as it has been foreseen or we will return to deal with you." She leapt back into the flame with that and the sky welcomed her as she flew away.

"Wow." She couldn't get the ring of that voice out of her head. She needed to sleep. She needed her strength for tomorrow. "Thank you for your time. Where can I sleep?"

Anwyn walked her and Seesee to one of the empty cottages. There were two beds and they were calling. "I will come get you at first light."

Abby already slept. She dreamed of Xander. His fingers, his hands, his smile and his body moving over hers. The blast of power that she woke to was no surprise.

Good thing, it was time to make war on a magus.

Chapter Forty-Nine

THE ENTIRE VILLAGE HAD TURNED OUT TO FACE THE ONCOMING threat. It was going to be quite the audience.

Terranor met her and, with the charge buzzing on her, she and Strykr had just said their morning greeting. The naked kind. Tough to do with so many kids around, but Terra had said the elders were always wishing to babysit.

They stood side by side as the forest lining began to rustle. Soon horses came forward, each carrying a battle-hardened warrior. At their head was the butt-head who had caused it all.

"Mervyn Atur, I presume." She heard gasps behind her and knew that the insult of dismissing his titles was a good call.

"What manner of ill-favoured wretch are you?" He had hair that was whitening around the sides and he simply let it flow. Not attractive, but not a spud either.

She turned to Terra. "He just called me ugly, didn't he?"

"Yes. In revenge for the insult no doubt."

"Gotcha." She took a deep breath. Time for the show to start. "You have something that does not belong to you."

"And what would that be?"

"The magic in your weapons. It was obtained by force and drawn out of a child just to create death and destruction." She stood and Terranor took her place at her side. "Today she will take it back."

Terranor concentrated and pulled on her magic.

Abby could see it start to flow to her, one tendril at a time. As she became more confident, the flow increased until it was a river of power that was working its way back to its originator.

She glowed with the power. It was beautiful to behold.

"No! She cannot do this. She has not been trained to do this!" Mervyn was panicking. It was a fine sight to behold.

"All weapons, which were enchanted, are no more. There is only one blade created that still has power and it resides far from here, only the most pure of heart can withdraw it. It lies beyond your grasp, Mervyn."

He was practically foaming at the mouth. "Then I shall take the Nexus and have her redo what she has undone."

"But which Nexus?" This was the show. She pulled her own magic to her, spurred on by remembering her dream last night. Power pushed at him, frightened the horses and had the army turning tail in moments. Terranor did the same on her side.

They turned to face each other and poured the energy into the pebbles they had started. The bubble of energy grew rapidly, their powers collided and swirled in a beautiful combination until a bubble covered the whole of the village. Terra and Abby inside, the army outside. Mervyn was shrieking and he ran toward them, sword upraised. And kept running right through them. He could not touch them. They were in a bubble out of time.

They watched him flail and scream at Terranor, his fury was palpable and when he began to gather his magic for an assault, the pixies went into action. He was surrounded by a cloud of whirling wings and giggling girls in a matter of seconds. When they finished their laughing tornado, they dissipated to the point where Abby could see the magus covered with a fine glittering powder. Pixie dust.

He screamed as the magic he had summoned was now trapped inside the veil of dust.

Abby looked to Terranor and stifled a laugh when she said, "Oh, that has to hurt."

"Did you design them to do that?"

"Not particularly, but I remember wishing that he could keep his magic to himself that day." She giggled.

It was a relief for Abby that Terra had not been broken by the experiences of her early life as a Nexus.

"I guess I put that into the pixies."

They turned from Mervyn railing and cursing at the discomfort of the confined power.

Abby smiled and hugged the first of her kind. "I guess you did."

"I do foresee one problem with them though." They were returning to her family and the astonished villagers who were looking out through the bubble of magic to the forest beyond.

"What is that?"

"I made them all girls. There won't be any more of them."

"That is a problem. Perhaps you could make more of them?"

"But they couldn't go through the bubble, could they?"

"Of course they could. Just like the elves and your kids can. The bubble will wrap them in your magic and they will be able to come and go as long as they don't all go at once. That would tear the bubble apart and leave you to the mercies of whoever was nearby." She tried to be matter of fact about it, but she didn't want Terra to mistake her lightness of delivery for lack of seriousness.

"I understand. And although you have not said it, I know that I will never leave this village. You are from the future, what have you seen for my children?" Her voice was choked with emotion, but she was doing what was best for her family and the friends who had taken her in.

"I don't know any specifics, but I do know that the magus who trained me looks so much like your Strykr that he could be his grandson. Your grandson. Or some form of descendent." At the sceptical look, she continued, "Seriously, when I came to and saw him there, I could have sworn that it was Xander."

"Really? You were trained by a magus and you still have your freedom?"

The villagers were touching the barrier and murmuring to themselves. Smiles were on their faces so it wasn't all bad.

"Really. The magical council created an equally represented, um, village for me. There is a werewolf, mermaid, the gorgon you have met, a magus, a vampire, I think, I haven't met him yet and there was one human who was trying to kill me. So it was a pretty safe environment for me to learn."

"You are serious? They let you roam free?"

"Yeah. Apparently, history has shown them that if they want the magic to continue to flow, they need to keep the Nexus from burning out. Our time is short on natural magic so my appearance was a big deal for them."

"How could your time be short on nature?"

"Humanity has over developed the planet. Too many cities and not enough green spaces. It stops nature from being able to assert itself."

"I am going to have a new respect for the forest nearby if this is true."

"Well, it won't happen for a few hundred years so you have some time." They were back at Terranor's cottage and the squealing excitement of the small girls flowed from the doorway and right to them.

Abby was shocked when the little hands reached for her as well, hugging at her legs and trying to get her to dance in a tight circle with them. The hands belonged to Elspeth, the little girl with the ancient eyes. Abby spun with her and eventually a laugh bubbled up. Power trickled from her as the other girls skipped and whirled with her.

She was so caught up in the dance and not tripping on the girls that she didn't realized they were moving to the center of the village. As they skipped and whirled, Abby caught short glimpses of Harby and the others forming a larger circle around them. There was so much laughter and giggling going on that when Abby's feet stepped on themselves and she went down, she let out a burst of energy that expanded and slammed into the inner side of the dome. "Aw, shit."

"Aunty Abby, did you do something bad?"

She was on the ground, covered in garden gnomes and had her hands over her eyes. "I don't know, Elspeth. You tell me."

"You had to do this so that when the magic fizzles, we can take it with us when we go into the world."

"Is that what I did?"

"Well, you weren't supposed to fall down. That was just funny."

Abby moved her fingers to see earnest blue eyes looking back at her.

"Really, Abby. This had to happen."

It all came slamming together. Her getting the book—it stimulating her creative drive. The gnomes having knowledge about using the book. The organization of her neighbourhood and the wise little five year old looking her in the eyes. "You did all this. You brought me here. Why?"

"To save my mom, my dad and my family. So that you could learn that history is never too far away. But mostly for my mom."

Abby sighed, absorbing it all. It wasn't too hard, she knew that someone was pulling her strings. "Then I am glad I came, but how do I get back?"

Elspeth cuddled against her, prompting her to sit up and cuddle back. "The door is still open. You never closed it. Just go back through the woods and you will hit your doorway."

"Well, aren't you just the most knowledgeable munchkin."

"I don't quite know what that means, but yes. Yes I am." A small giggle turned to hoots of laughter.

Abby tickled her small victim into acting like a little girl again. The other little ladies started to play, too, and Abby carefully pulled herself free of the writhing tickling pile. When the gnomes joined in, she just shook her head. She made her way back to Terranor's cottage and was met with a surprise.

Anwyn was writing and Seesee was dictating. It took Abby a while to catch on, but it was *her* story that was being told. She looked over to Terranor, but she was listening to the tale with rapt attention. Heaving a deep sigh, Abby took a seat and let the tale of her last three weeks unfold.

Chapter Fifty

"Seesee, the story is lovely but we have to go home now. The gargoyles are missing their evening appearance on television." She was trying to make light of the situation, but it fell flat. They needed to go back to their own time.

"You are right. I had to record this moment in the Eternal Archive though. It was where I first read of you, Abby, and where I knew that I must do whatever it took to be selected for Oak Point."

"Including..." The assignation with the minotaur went unsaid. "You are a good friend, Seesee, and a better baker. I am glad you came with me to this place."

"You are?"

"Your companionship was welcome as was your talent for public speaking. Not to mention the poisoned ivy." She gave her a bright grin and watched her dusky skin flush bronze again.

Terra looked between them and then turned to ask Abby an earnest question, "Abby, is it true?"

"Is what true Terra?"

"That you came to your power less than one month ago?"

She looked at her host and thought her answer out carefully. "I came in to my powers late, I am beyond my thirtieth year. The first weeks of my power were wracked with trials and attempts on my life. It was there that I learned the tricks that I have shown you here. The more you use your talents for creation or defence, the stronger they will be."

"If I had but a third of your power, I would have done away with the magus years ago."

"And you would have been hunted to death by the council for

killing one of their own. Your daughters would never have been and Strykr would either have never met you or died in your defence. Nothing would have brought your family back."

Those were the words she needed to hear. Terranor broke, sobbing in Abby's arms. Babbling about her family, the power that wouldn't come, the hate that she bore the magus and a thousand other thoughts that had poisoned her for years.

Elspeth stood in the doorway to the cottage and gave Abby a watery smile over her mother's sobbing shoulder. This was the final reason for the visit. To release her mother from the guilt that had weighed on her.

Anwyn and Seesee left them alone, conversing in low tones as they moved into the village proper.

"Terranor. Things in our past make us the beings that we are today. They shape the creatures that we create, and that includes your children. Mourn for those lost in bringing you to this point, but go boldly after all that you want in this life from here on in. The past is set, even my coming was arranged, but the future is yours to shape." Abby recognized the truth of her words as they passed her lips. "I think I am going to have to follow my own advice." She gave the teary Nexus a kiss on the forehead. "I have to go and see to my own future now."

"Then thank you for your past." A small jolt of magic flowed through her as their hands touched. "And blessings for your future."

The trip back through the open portal was as smooth as the first.

"Ow, ow, ow, ow. Fucking ow." The way back through the woods had been hampered slightly by lurking members of the magus' army. The brownies cleared the way though, jumping from trees and setting the men to clawing themselves free of their armour.

Abby sent the gargoyles through first, then Seesee and finally her gnomes as she brought up the rear. She had to pull the bubble shut behind them so she had to be the final one to go through. It had caused quite a stir, but eventually she simply launched the gnomes through bodily.

It was a scowling collection of gnomes that greeted her when she came to. "Sorry, guys. But you can't close the portal without me. And it would have made no sense for me to jump and leave you there."

They looked at each other for a long moment before Bitsy nodded sharply and jerked his head to the kitchen. They straightened dented hats and strutted into the dining area.

Abby turned her head on the carpet to see the gargoyles had made it back to the yard and were once again heading for town. "Aw crap. Where did I leave that remote?"

Seesee was sitting up and rubbing her head, tendrils of her hair rubbing at her temples. "That is not the most comfortable way to travel. I think I will stick to pogo sticking through the woods. It is less jarring."

"You may have a point there." Groaning, Abby sat up and rapidly disassembled the transportation device. She took the book and put it in the safest place she knew. The centre of her bed. With Xander out of town, no one would think to look in her bedroom. Upon returning to her living room where Seesee was slumped on the couch, she had to ask, "So do we tell anyone?"

Seesee's hair shook in the negative. "No. Those who need to know of our journey already know. I have known of it since I was twenty and now I am at peace with how it turned out. I will not mention it again."

"Fine. We left for a shopping trip to the states. Are you good with that?"

"First you might want to look at how long we were gone." She pointed to the television. The weather channel had the date and time displayed and it was the same day that they had left.

"Well, hell. Time travel is tricky."

"What a fabulous understatement." The grin was infectious and, as the gnomes brought them a light snack, they sat giggling and sniggering at the ridiculousness of the situation.

Time travel. Holy crap.

Chapter Fifty-One

"ABBY, ARE YOU HOME?" XANDER'S PERFUNCTORY KNOCK preceded him by only a second.

Scrambling, Abby turned off the television and hid the remote between the cushions of the sofa. Watching *home movies* of her guys was becoming a guilty pleasure now that she knew money was coming to heal their naughtiness. The advance cheque was on its way. She got to her feet and greeted him with a gentle hug. "Hiya, sweetie. How are you feeling? How was transporting Randy for you? How did the council take the briefing?"

His wrists were still raw where he had fought the handcuffs. They had scabbed over lightly, but were still red and raw. Almost like he was reacting to the metal and not the confinement method.

"They are satisfied to leave you in my tutelage for the time being. I think they are a little afraid of you if you can believe that. They don't know you like I do, kitten." He returned her hug softly. "And how are you doing? Any power surges that I should know about? Any reaction to our communications through the mirror?"

"I am completely recovered. Nothing odd whatsoever." Well, it wasn't odd. It was normal for Abby. Or at least what passed for normal. She was doomed or blessed to jettison magic when she was horny. She would just have to deal with it.

He looked into her eyes, his scepticism shining through. "Are you completely sure? There has been nothing unusual happening?"

"Nope. Everything is completely normal around here." She carefully did not mention yesterday's episode where she found the white shirt that he had left on his first time over. Just one inhalation and her hormones had shifted into overdrive. She had missed him and wanted him so much in that one moment that the iron of her fireplace dogs had formed curly cue hearts and her teapot had whistled at her. The 1812 overture to be precise.

She also skipped over meeting the first Nexus and what had to be his ancestor, light deceptions that wouldn't harm anyone.

The news report she had just been watching had let her know that she had reached out beyond her home. She was just hoping that he didn't know. The smug sureness in his eyes shook her belief that no one had noticed.

With a practiced gesture, the remote flew from between the cushions to land in his hand. He turned on the television and watched the last bit of the report.

"So as the video shows, the pink flamingos that recently decorated the yards on Brandon Street have come to life, formed a flock and begun migrating to the south. This reporter has no idea where they are headed, or how they animated themselves, but this is just another example of the local color that has taken over the small town of Sargent. Perhaps the mysterious woman will shed some light on this, if she ever decides to come forward. If you know her, please call..."

The screen went black.

"Okay, so I slipped up. I missed you and dug out the shirt that you gave me, well that I had the gnomes take from your house. It smelled like you and, well...you can figure out the rest." A blush was rioting across her cheeks.

"Anything else? Have the gnomes been under control?" He flopped onto the couch and tugged her down onto his lap.

She repositioned herself carefully, not wanting a repeat of the first time. He had recovered manfully, but best not tempt fate. "Well, they have been as much under my control as they ever were. Mitsy and Harbinger are, uh, hitting it off on a more personal level and I have occasionally managed to get clothing on Skint. But that is more trouble than it is worth and I think he and one of my gargoyles are hitting it off."

He closed his eyes and leaned his head on the back of the couch. "Gargoyle?"

"Yeah, my agent asked for a new book so I figured instead of more gnomes, that this one would be about gargoyles. Buffy is my prototype. Angel and Firefly are the secondaries."

"Do you have a title yet? I mean for your new book?"

"Of course. I always have a title before I start. I know what to call everything at every stage in the game." She was trying to be coy, but given his obvious arousal under her thigh, coy was overkill. The direct approach might work. "Well, Xander. Since you are here, you may as well shield me while I produce a little more magic."

"How are you planning to do that?"

"Oh, I just figured I would improvise." Using the back of the couch for leverage, she raised her hips and moved around until she was straddling him. Her body began to tingle the instant that she started to move and his warding snapped into action around them. A giggle broke from her lips. "Nice reflexes."

"Around you, I need every reflex I have."

His dark eyes sparkled as he raised his hips into hers. She smiled back and rubbed against him with catlike thoroughness. It was on her third rub that their lips locked. The instant that she touched her lips with his, a burst of power shook his wards. She pulled back and blushed. "Uh, sorry. It's been a while."

His hands held her hips tight to his. "Don't apologize. It's your nature. And as reflexes go, I am sure that the creatures you have brought to life are appreciative. Where are they by the way?"

"Out back. I bought them a keg." Her lips found the pulse point at the base of his throat and she licked it delicately, loving the way he shook under her at the tiny touch.

Her words obviously took a moment to sink in. "Wait. You bought them a keg? You knew I was coming?"

She sighed at the double entendre. "These new senses are good for something. I was monitoring the power levels around the Sargent area. I could sense when you came through and headed home."

"You can track me?"

"Not exactly. But I know the flavour of your magic."

He had set her back from him and her mood was rapidly deteriorating. She crossed her arms over her breasts and tried to calm her racing heart.

"So you can feel the magic of others and even track people with it?"

"Well, if I know the feel of their power. Like I do yours. Probably. I guess. I don't know." She carefully climbed off him and crossed the room. Analytical discussion of her newfound talent was not exactly arousing. She was too scared of her power to enjoy talking about it. His footsteps followed her through the house and to the sliding doors overlooking her deck.

The gnomes were enjoying their tiny kegger.

Xander's arms came around her. She snuggled back and breathed deeply of the same scent that had reminded her of him days earlier. Her head leaned back against his shoulder and she sighed. This was her world now. Her weird little world. With the gnomes of suburbia and all the creatures that lived on magic. Her magic.

Music started behind them, the CD player belting out a snazzy tango. His whisper came to her on the wind, "Care to dance?"

Author's Note

Gnomes of Suburbia is the first of the Nexus Chronicles. There are currently two more books directly involving Abby planned and a few spinoffs are also in the works.

Thanks for joining me in Oak Point Way, I hope you had fun and it inspires you to look at the average lawn ornament with a bit of respect, or fear, or amusement.

And remember, *Always remember where your pants are.*

Viola Grace
http://www.violagrace.com

Look for these and other books by Viola Grace at:

www.devinedestinies.com

Freak Factor - Sector Guard book 1

Living life on Kaddaka station was predictable and profitable. Mala's talent for undetectable repairs has made her quite wealthy and the station quite popular. When a Reflex ship comes in hot, out of control and unable to stop, she is the woman for the job. The job itself is an audition for the Sector Guard, but unless Mala is successful the passengers of the ship will never be able to tell her the good news.

Isabi has been less than enthusiastic about meeting his new partner, until he sees her. Suddenly his interest is peaked. She doesn't seem to notice the pheromones that he exudes and she certainly doesn't fawn all over him. This woman may be worthy of her position as his partner, and he will not have her working with anyone else. Their talents make them the perfect team, now he just has to prove it to her.

Made in the USA